THE HISTORICAL HOUSE

This series is a unique collaboration between three
award-winning authors, Adèle Geras, Linda Newbery
and Ann Turnbull, all writing about one very special
house and the extraordinary young women
who have lived there throughout history.

THE HISTORICAL HOUSE

ADÈLE GERAS
Lizzie's Wish

Cecily's Portrait

ↅ

LINDA NEWBERY
Polly's March

Andie's Moon

ↅ

ANN TURNBULL
Josie Under Fire

Mary Ann & Miss Mozart

LINDA NEWBERY

Polly's March

USBORNE

For Megan, of course

First published in 2004 by Usborne Publishing Ltd., Usborne House,
83-85 Saffron Hill, London EC1N 8RT, England.
www.usborne.com

Copyright © Linda Newbery, 2004.
The right of Linda Newbery to be identified as the author of this work has been
asserted by her in accordance with the Copyright, Designs and Patents Act, 1988.

Cover photography: Suffragettes and Votes for Women © Mary Evans Picture Library. Girl
on swing © Hutton Archive/Getty Images. Girl on right © Sylvia Trevelyan.
Inside illustrations by Ian McNee.

The name Usborne and the devices ♀ 🎈 are Trade Marks of Usborne Publishing Ltd.

A CIP catalogue record for this book is available from the British Library.

FMAMJJASOND/07

ISBN 9780746060315

Printed in India.

Contents

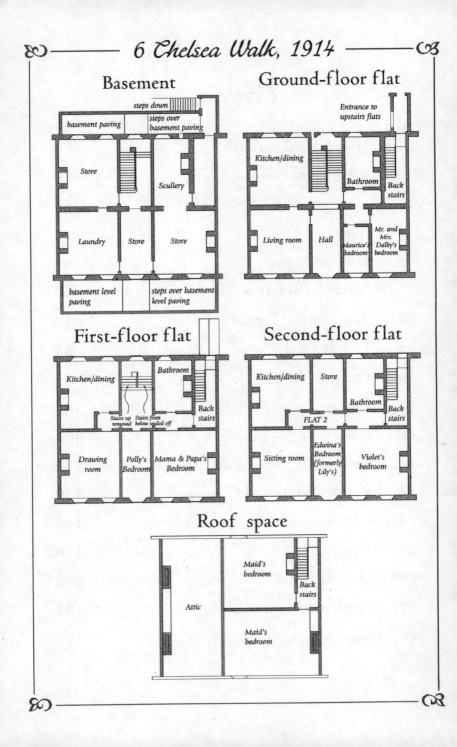

6 Chelsea Walk, 1914

Basement

steps down

basement paving

steps over basement paving

Store

Scullery

Laundry

Store

Store

basement level paving

steps over basement level paving

Ground-floor flat

Entrance to upstairs flats

Kitchen/dining

Bathroom

Back stairs

Living room

Hall

Maurice's bedroom

Mr. and Mrs. Dalby's bedroom

First-floor flat

Kitchen/dining

Bathroom

Back stairs

Stairs up removed

Stairs from below sealed off

Drawing room

Polly's Bedroom

Mama & Papa's Bedroom

Second-floor flat

Kitchen/dining

Store

Bathroom

Back stairs

FLAT 2

Sitting room

Edwina's Bedroom (formerly Lily's)

Violet's bedroom

Roof space

Maid's bedroom

Back stairs

Attic

Maid's bedroom

Chapter One

New Neighbours

The swing tree had always been Polly's favourite part of the garden. She came here to sit, or to read, or to watch the birds squabbling over thrown bread; or she came to swing. She liked to push herself as high as she could, her stretched-out feet pointing at Lily's bedroom on the second floor, till she almost felt she could launch herself from the swing seat and land neatly on the mat beside Lily's bed.

But now it wasn't Lily's bedroom, not any more, and today Polly couldn't find the energy for proper swinging.

Until last week, she and Lily had come here together – to be by themselves, to talk and giggle and share secrets. Now there was no Lily, no one to share anything, and Polly didn't even want to look up at the top-floor flat. For nearly a week, the windows had been blank and empty. Today the new people were moving in, and they were going to be duller than dull, she just knew it. It was so unfair!

Polly sat glumly, twisting the swing seat one way, then the other. She dragged her feet on the scuffed bare earth underneath.

She and Lily had been best friends for seven years, ever since Polly and her parents had moved into Number Six, Chelsea Walk. As their mothers were good friends too, Polly and Lily had shared a nanny and attended the same school; they had walked along the Thames Embankment and picnicked in Ranelagh

Gardens; they both had piano lessons with Lily's Aunt Dorothy, who lived nearby. Now Lily's mother was ill, and the family had moved to Tunbridge Wells, where the healthy air would do her good, Dr. Mayes said. All Lily's family's possessions and furniture had been carried out, less than a week ago.

This afternoon, Polly had arrived home from school to find a van parked outside, and boxes and crates being carried in by the very same men, three of them, in flat caps. What a strange job it must be, Polly thought – carting people's whole lives from one place to the next, swapping people around like books on shelves! She felt resentful of the newcomers. There hadn't been time to get used to Lily being gone, let alone to face the thought of new people moving in, putting their own pictures and ornaments where Lily's had been, making it all different.

"Lily can come to stay, sometimes," Polly's mother had said yesterday, seeing her gloomy face. "Tunbridge Wells isn't that far away. You haven't said goodbye to her for ever and ever. And there's still Maurice!"

Maurice! Grown-ups simply didn't understand. As if Maurice could even begin to replace Lily! Polly glowered at the windows of the Dalbys' ground-floor flat. Polly's mother and Mrs. Dalby often had afternoon tea together or sat chatting while they sewed, but that didn't mean Polly was going to be friends with Horrid Maurice. He was the worst boy she knew. As she knew very few boys, this was less of an insult than she'd have liked; but she felt sure that even if she knew hundreds and hundreds, Maurice would still be the one she detested most.

If ever he saw Polly and Lily playing in the garden, he used to come out purely to pester them. He was the same age as them, twelve; but as Lily remarked loftily, "He's only a boy. They always seem younger than girls for their age." Once, he'd sneaked up behind Polly with a toad he'd found at the end of the garden, holding it so close that she came face to face with it when she turned round, and couldn't help shrieking with horror. That piercing shriek – she hadn't known she could make such a sound – had annoyed her as much as it had amused Maurice; she never usually made a fuss about mice, spiders or other crawly creatures. Another time, he had thrown Eugenie, Lily's doll, high into the branches of the walnut tree, where her long hair had become so firmly snagged on twigs that Polly had to call the gardener to bring a ladder and climb to the rescue.

Why couldn't it have been *Maurice's* mother who was ill and needed the Tunbridge Wells air?

And now a new disappointment! The one hope remaining to Polly was that the new occupants of Flat Three would have a daughter her own age – not, of course, one she would like as much as Lily, because that would be disloyal, but still someone who could fill the friend gap. But Papa had heard that the new people weren't a family at all, but a pair of spinsters: Miss Cross and Miss Rutherford. Polly wrinkled her nose when she heard the names. She imagined the

Misses Cross and Rutherford as elderly ladies, dressed stiffly in black and purple and old lace that smelled of mothballs. Miss Cross would be cross, of course – probably they both would. They'd look down long noses at her and would sniff in disapproval if she played in the garden. They'd be hard of hearing and would cup their hands to their ears if she tried to speak to them, so that she'd have to repeat everything three times. They might even be so deaf as to use ear trumpets. Yet their ears would be sharply tuned to any noise she made on the back stairs or in her bedroom; there would be complaints to Mama and Papa. She knew it! She disliked them already.

"Oh, but this is lovely!" said a voice, close behind her.

Polly turned. Two people had come out of the doorway that led to the back stairs: both young women, dressed alike in navy-blue skirts and white blouses. The taller and thinner of the two was looking this way and that, giving excited little claps of her hands; the other, dark-haired, stocky and hatless, gazed around her as she came down the steps to the grass.

"We could hardly have done better!" the tall one went on. "And look, this tree – lovely shade on a hot day – oh! Hello! I'm so sorry if we startled you."

They were coming towards her, smiling and interested, as if a girl on a swing were the most exciting thing they could hope to find in a garden. Polly felt annoyed with herself; she could have dodged out of sight behind the blackcurrant bushes, to look and listen without being seen.

Slowly, she got up from the swing seat, and tugged at her skirt. "Only for a moment." She looked from one face to the other. These two must be nieces, or something, of the old ladies who were moving in; spinsters, of course, wouldn't have daughters or grand-daughters.

"You live here, do you?" the shorter one asked.

"Yes. Up there, in the middle flat." Polly pointed to the first-floor windows.

"Then we're going to be neighbours!" exclaimed the tall young woman, who seemed ready to be delighted by everything. "How marvellous! We must introduce ourselves properly. How do you do? I'm Edwina Rutherford, and this is Violet Cross." She held out a hand to shake Polly's. "Do tell us who you are!"

"Oh!" Polly was unable to hide her surprise. "But you're not – I mean, I thought – I thought you'd be cross and old!" It came out, just like that, before she could stop herself; she blushed at her rudeness.

Miss Rutherford laughed, not seeming to mind. "I *feel* old, sometimes. *Look* old, sometimes." And Polly noticed that her face, under her hat brim, looked pale and drawn, like that of a very ill person who was venturing out for the first time after weeks on a sickbed. "As for Violet –" Miss Rutherford turned to her friend – "Cross by name, kindly by nature!"

"And your name?" prompted Miss Cross.

"Polly. Paulina Elizabeth Genevieve Stubbs, but I'm

always called Polly. So you're really the people moving in upstairs?"

Miss Rutherford laughed. "We really are. We've come outside to give ourselves a rest from boxes and dust and decisions. Maybe you could show us around the garden?"

Polly wasn't sure what to show them that they couldn't see easily for themselves, but she said, "Yes, of course." Miss Rutherford made a big show of setting off on a Grand Tour, adjusting her hat, looking round expectantly, and putting her best foot forward.

"Now, Edwina," said Miss Cross, glancing anxiously at her, "you're not to go over-tiring yourself. It's been a long day. You ought to be putting your feet up. The doctor said—"

"I can rest later," Miss Rutherford assured her. But she took the offered arm, and leaned slightly against her friend as they took a few steps down the garden. Only a few steps, because Polly wanted them to have a proper look at the tree. She stood back to gaze up at it, its cracked bark and the spreading canopy of leaves, and the branch that had the swing's ropes lashed round it.

"We'll start here. This tree," she said proudly, "is a walnut tree. We get walnuts from it in autumn. The Romans, you know, brought walnuts when they came to England, and planted them. This one was grown from a walnut by a girl who lived here years and years ago. And now it's big enough to swing from!"

"How marvellous!" Miss Rutherford tilted back her head to look at the upper branches. "And how do you know that?"

"Mrs. Parks told me. She's our cook."

"Imagine!" said Miss Rutherford. "One little walnut, growing into a tree this size! I shall find a nut in autumn and try to grow a new tree myself. There," she added, looking sidelong at Miss Cross, "you see what great things can grow from small beginnings! What an inspiration, to look out of our window and see this every day!"

"You got more'n enough inspiration if you ask me," said Miss Cross, almost crossly.

Polly looked at them with interest. She had thought at first that they might be cousins, but now decided that they couldn't be related at all; they looked so unalike, and their voices were very different, too. Whereas Miss Rutherford spoke in the clear, carrying tone of most people who lived in this part of Chelsea, Miss Cross's way of speaking was less refined – the way a servant might speak. Polly liked her friendly directness, but her accent was what Mama called ·common. Polly wondered if maybe she was looking after Miss Rutherford – perhaps she was a paid nurse, or companion. Miss Rutherford had the liveliest blue eyes, that seemed to dart around taking in everything; but she also looked as tired as a candle on its last sputter. Her skin looked almost transparent, there were shadows under her eyes, and she was so thin that – as Mama would say – a puff of wind would blow her over. And Miss Cross had mentioned the doctor, and resting. Mama saw the doctor quite often, and was supposed to rest each afternoon with her feet up on the couch, but that was because of the new baby that was on the way. That couldn't possibly be the cause of Miss Rutherford's frailness.

"Excuse me, Miss Rutherford –" Polly ventured.

"Oh, please – call me Edwina, and Violet, Violet! Miss Rutherford makes me feel like an elderly spinster! You don't want us to call you Miss Stubbs, do you? May we call you Polly?"

"Yes, of course. Well, er – Edwina," Polly continued awkwardly, not used to calling grown-ups by their first names, "I hope you won't think I'm rude, but are you ill?"

"Well, like –" Miss Cross, Violet, began, but Edwina cut her short, fixing Polly with her straight blue gaze.

"Yes, Polly, in a way I have been ill. You see, I've just been released from prison."

Chapter Two

A Letter to Lily

...Sports Day, and an outing to Kew, but it isn't nearly as much fun without you, Polly wrote, forming the letters carefully. *Whenever we have partners I have to go with Maudie Marchant, just because no one else wants to. I call her Moody Marchant.*

She was at the dining table, supposedly doing her French preparation. The writing paper – smooth cream bond, with *Flat 2, 6 Chelsea Walk* printed in curling script – rested on the pages of her French book, so that it could be hidden if Mama came unexpectedly into the room. As Mrs. Dalby was here, and she and Mama were having tea in the drawing room, Polly knew she was safe as long as she could hear the two alternating voices; if the conversation stopped and footsteps came this way, there would be time to hide the letter and pretend to be concentrating very hard on French conjugations.

But something very exciting has happened, Polly wrote on, *and it's to do with the new people in your flat!* She hesitated – would this make Lily feel she had been too easily replaced? She thought, gazed at the piano, and wrote again. *It won't be the same as having you here, but they are not the two prim old ladies I expected. Their names are Edwina Rutherford and Violet Cross, and they want to be friends. I don't mean friends like you and me, they are too old for that, but friendly, anyway. They have already told me all sorts of things! It is hard to tell how old they are – grown-up, but not very. Anyway, they are much younger than my mama or yours. And, you'll never guess –*

Miss McFarlane at school said that a sentence should never begin with *and*, but sometimes it seemed just right. Polly stopped writing again and leaned her chin on her hand, looking out into the branches of the walnut tree. At this height, on the first floor, it filled the window with green. Amazing, the way it branched and branched, so that from up here Polly had a squirrel's-eye view, looking through the mass of leaves, each one divided into seven leaflets, with the dangling, catkin-like flowers that made the whole tree seem decorated for summer. Papa had talked about getting it cut down, complaining that it was too tall for the garden and too close to the house and that it blocked the light, but Polly and Mama had argued passionately that it must stay. Most houses had gardens, but not every house had its own walnut tree! And Papa enjoyed eating the walnuts at Christmas, and having them pickled for the rest of the year. Mrs. Parks, the cook-housekeeper, had her own special way of pickling, which Papa said was better than anyone else's.

Polly's mind flicked back to the thrilling moment when Edwina announced that she'd been in prison. Prison! Polly had felt her mouth opening in a fish-like gape. Only very bad people went to prison, didn't they? Edwina looked and sounded so ladylike that Polly couldn't begin to imagine what crime she might have committed.

Violet had laughed. "You ought to be more careful about coming straight out with things," she told her friend. "Look how you've shocked Polly now! Don't worry," she told Polly, "she's not a thief or a murderer!"

"No, I didn't think –" Polly faltered, unsure what she *did* think. "But, then, what did you –?"

"I was sent to Holloway Prison for attacking a policeman outside Buckingham Palace." For a moment,

Edwina looked even taller, and her eyes fiercer.

"Attacking – oh! You're a –" Newspaper headlines flashed into Polly's head; she thought of her father reading *The Times* at breakfast, shaking his head at what the world was coming to. "You're one of those suffragettes!"

Edwina nodded. "I am. And very proud of it."

According to Papa, it was completely disgraceful; ladies getting up to such antics, as he called them. How exciting, though, Polly thought: How brave, to shout in the streets and confront the police and not be told what to do! How marvellous to be so *unladylike*! Being ladylike all the time must be very, very dull.

"Are you one, too?" she asked Violet. "A suffragette?"

She noticed the quick glance that passed between the two young women: the faintest suggestion of a smile from Edwina, a tightening of the lips and tilt of the head from Violet. Then Violet answered:

"I'm a campaigner for votes for women, yes. Votes

for everyone. I prefer suffragist to suffragette. Let's just say, Edwina and me don't always see eye to eye on getting our points made. I don't go round thumping policemen, for a start, nor throwing myself under racehorses, neither. Edwina, she'd do it soon as cross the road."

"You didn't –?"

"Of course not," Edwina said, smiling. Then her face became serious. "Violet was referring to Emily Davison, our brave comrade who sacrificed herself to the Cause last summer."

Polly remembered that – the news vendors shouting in the streets, the front-page headlines. Emily Davison – Polly had forgotten the name – had gone to the Derby race meeting, and waited by the side of the track for the horses' thundering approach; then she had run out into the path of the King's own horse.

Now, at the table, Polly sat screwing and unscrewing the top of her pen, thinking about it, imagining herself as Emily Davison. What must she have been feeling?

Merging with the crowd, feigning an interest in the race itself and which horse was likely to win – and all the time steeling herself for the moment of breaking free, ducking under the rails for that wild dash under the horses' flailing limbs. She had been killed – not immediately, but had been kicked and trampled so badly that she died in hospital a few days later. Was that what she intended? And, having died, she would never know if women *did* get the vote, or whether they had to go on and on chaining themselves to railings, smashing windows, slashing paintings in galleries...

"Was it awful in prison?" Polly had asked Edwina, looking at her with a renewed shyness. It felt almost like talking to someone who had died, and come back to tell her about it.

Violet answered first. "Needn't have been as awful as Edwina made it. She refused to eat. Went on hunger strike. You'll have read about it in the papers, I 'spect. She's done all that before, course. Nearly starved herself to death, she did, till they stuck a feeding tube down her neck." She darted a look at her friend. "Now the government's got a new way of dealing with it," she told Polly. "P'raps you know. No more force-feeding – no, they let the women starve themselves till they're fit to collapse. Then they let them out, but only till they've got enough strength to be arrested again."

"So you might have to go back to prison?" Polly said, in a small voice. Part of her mind was working on a new problem: *What will Mama and Papa say?*

"Not only might, but *will*," Edwina said, with what Polly already recognized as her stubborn look. "Cat and Mouse, it's called. You've seen the way a cat plays with a mouse, like a toy – letting it run, then clawing it back again? That's what the prison authorities are doing to us – playing with us, treating us as their victims! But one thing I can tell you, Polly, is – we will never give up the fight, never! Not till women have the same rights as men!"

Polly didn't think she had ever met anyone as

determined as Edwina. Ill as she was, she seemed to burn with passion, her whole body trembling with it.

"Come on in now." Violet tugged at her friend's arm. "You're over-tired. You won't mind showing us the garden another time, will you, Polly? Time's getting on, there's still a lot to do."

"Please don't fuss! I'm perfectly well!" Edwina retorted. But she seemed to sag and become smaller, as if the last blaze of energy had been snuffed out. "All right, then. Just a little rest, before we unpack the books. Polly, I'm so glad we've made friends!" she added, finding the energy for a cheery wave. "You must come up and visit us when we're shipshape!"

Polly watched them go back across the grass and in at the side door that led to the upper flats, Violet helping Edwina, who lifted her skirt with one hand and placed her feet very carefully on the step, like a doddery old lady. Inside, there were two staircases to be climbed to the top flat. Lily and Polly used to bound up two at a time when no one was around to tell them off, but it would be a long climb for someone as weak as Edwina.

New friends! Had she really made new friends? How amazing that people so much older, and with such important things to do, should take notice of *her*!

She unscrewed her pen, and wrote: *They are suffragettes! They don't seem to agree on how to go about it, but one of them, Edwina, has actually been in prison and been on hunger strike, and —*

"Polly?"

Mama's voice in the hallway. Quickly, Polly slipped the letter between the pages of her French book and pretended to be aroused from deep thought.

"Yes, Mama?"

"You must be nearly finished, surely? Do come and join us."

Polly closed her books and went through to the drawing room, ushered by her mother. Mrs. Dalby, Maurice's mother, was sitting in a chair and half-turned towards the window; the tea tray was on a low table in front of her, and one of Mrs. Parks' special strawberry sponge cakes, sprinkled with icing sugar.

"Hello, Polly. You're such a good girl, doing your prep so diligently!" said Mrs. Dalby, in the cooing voice Polly found so irritating. "Now do tell me." She sat forward, hands on her knees. "Maurice told me he saw you talking to our new neighbours, a little while ago! I'm just eaten up with curiosity – do tell me everything you've found out!"

Chapter Three

Gossip

"Oh, not much, really," Polly said cautiously. Trust nosy old Maurice to have been watching! Not that there was anything wrong with talking in the garden, was there?

Mama, passing Polly a slice of cake, gave her a sidelong look. "You've spoken to them? Why ever didn't you tell me, when you came indoors?"

"Two young ladies, Maurice said. Are they sisters?" probed Mrs. Dalby.

"No, not sisters. Their names are Edwina Rutherford and Violet Cross."

"And where have they come from?"

Polly flicked a glance at Mrs. Dalby, then at her mother, tempted to say, "From Holloway Prison." Straightening the smile that twitched at her mouth, she replied instead, "I don't know. We only talked for a few moments, and it was mainly about – about the walnut tree."

"Didn't you find out anything about them at all?" said Mrs. Dalby, looking quite crestfallen. "Are they young women of private means? Presumably their families are renting the flat for them? I shouldn't imagine they'd be working girls, would you, Catherine?" she asked Polly's mother. "There's a maid, my Elsie told me – living in one of the attic rooms."

"I shall invite them to tea!" declared Mama. "Then we'll meet them properly – find out all about them. Early next week, I shall suggest – when they've had time to settle themselves. You must come as well, Meredith!"

Polly felt uneasy. She wanted to keep her new friends to herself.

"I'd be delighted," said Mrs. Dalby. "After all, we ought to know who's living under our roof. But I really must be going." She got to her feet, straightened her skirt and adjusted the lace collar of her blouse. "Polly, do come down and play chess with Maurice if you get lonely – I know how badly you must be missing Lily. Now, Catherine, my dear, make sure you look after yourself." She patted Mama's arm. "Not too much standing, remember! I'm sure I've told you, when I was expecting Maurice, how dreadfully my ankles swelled? Rest every afternoon with my feet up, that's what the doctor advised, but of course I'm far too active for that. You must be so excited, Polly! Not much longer to wait. Such fun it'll be, having a little brother."

Polly swallowed a mouthful of cake. "How do you know it'll be a brother?"

"Well, or sister. But –" Mrs. Dalby touched Mama's arm again, and gave her a twinkling look. "But I have a feeling it's a boy this time, and my feelings rarely let me down! Goodbye, then. Goodbye, dear." And at last she was gone, in a waft of lily-of-the-valley.

Mama rang the bell for Mrs. Parks to come for the tea things. She stood up in the awkward way she had developed since becoming so large; she stifled a yawn, and put a hand to the small of her back. "I really do think I'd better lie down and rest before dinner. Do make sure you put your things away, won't you, darling? You know how Papa hates to see things lying around. Did you finish your prep?"

"Nearly," said Polly. "Mama, do *you* hope the new baby's going to be a boy?"

Mama looked at her. "Well, of course it would be lovely to have one of each! And Papa would be thrilled to have a son. But we shall both be delighted, whichever it is."

"Wasn't Papa thrilled when I was born? Was he disappointed?"

"Polly!" Mama touched Polly's hair, smoothing back a wayward strand that escaped from its pigtail. "No one was disappointed, of course not – you know we couldn't love you more, both of us! But you have to understand that there's a special thing about fathers and sons. A son, you see, will keep our name, and will marry and have children and grandchildren. Whereas you'll change your name when you get married, just as I did, and your children will have your husband's name, not Stubbs."

"Supposing I don't meet someone I want to marry?"

Mama laughed, and patted her shoulder. "Darling, of course you will! When you're old enough, you'll meet all sorts of suitable young men. Some young man will come along, don't you worry, who will think himself very lucky indeed! If you tidy up your things, there'll be time for your piano practice – there's a good girl. Dinner will be at six."

Polly went back to the dining table, her letter and her French prep, still thinking about her shadowy future husband. Mama hadn't really answered her question. Polly hadn't asked whether anyone would want to marry her; she had been wondering whether she would meet someone she might *choose*. It wasn't the same thing. Anyway, Polly wanted to be an explorer. She wanted to travel the world and see all sorts of places and people. There wouldn't be time for a husband, unless he was an explorer as well.

She couldn't imagine Edwina Rutherford waiting for some nice, suitable young man to come along and think himself very lucky. Nor Violet Cross.

Supposing the only suitable young man she met turned out to be Maurice? She'd sooner marry a duck-billed platypus, she thought, opening her French book at the page where the letter was hidden; she'd sooner marry a wart hog. Lily, who had recently been to her cousin's wedding, had told Polly that in the marriage service, the bride had to promise to obey her husband. That meant doing whatever he told you, the way Mama always did what Papa said. Really, you might as well stay on at school, if someone was going to carry on telling you what to do and not do.

Imagine promising that to someone as slimy as Maurice! Polly unscrewed her pen lid and stuck out her tongue, pulling the sort of face Mrs. Parks said she should avoid, in case the wind changed and she got stuck like it. She'd rather marry a *toad*.

Chapter Four

Slug

"Can you imagine," Polly said to Maudie Marchant at morning break, "wanting something so badly that you'd die for it?"

Maudie finished chomping a mouthful of apple before answering. "No," she said at last. "If you were dead, what would be the point?"

"You might want something for someone else," Polly explained, "not just for yourself."

Maudie considered this possibility, nibbling round the apple core till it was little more than an extension of its stalk. "No. I can't think of anything I'd want *that* much. Can you?"

If Polly were honest, the answer would have been no; but instead she asked, "What about the suffragettes – you know, getting sent to prison and going on hunger strike?"

"Oh, *them*." Maudie had eaten all there was to eat of the apple, but instead of flicking the core into the bushes at the edge of the playground, as Polly would have done, she held it carefully by the stalk, no doubt waiting to put it in the litter bin on the way back to the classroom: Maudie did everything according to the rules. "My father says they're just vandals and hooligans. Lock them up and throw away the key, that's what he says. Have them horsewhipped. If they behave like gangs of ruffians, making trouble in the streets, how do they *expect* to get the vote?"

Polly was silent for a moment. Her father said

exactly the same sort of thing, tutting as he read the newspaper, reading out bits to Mama. He seemed to think that the campaigning women belonged to an entirely different species from his wife, who sat demurely with her needlework, nodding and agreeing with whatever he said. What was Papa going to say when he found out that two suffragettes (or one suffragette and one suffragist: Polly was unclear about the distinction) were living in the very same house, sharing his roof? What would he say about Mama inviting them to tea? Perhaps, Polly thought, she ought to warn them; tell them to keep quiet, and talk only about the weather and the latest fashions and other polite, everyday things. Or perhaps it would be better if they didn't come at all, if they just smiled politely and said *How do you do?* to anyone they met on the way in or out.

In the classroom, Polly paused by the globe on the window table to play her favourite game. She made it spin on its stem as fast as it would go; then she closed her eyes, touched a finger to the whirling surface – but not hard enough to slow its turning – and waited for it to come to a complete stop. Then she looked at where her finger was resting, and thought: *That's where I might go, one day, when I can go anywhere I like.* It felt a bit like someone telling her fortune by reading a crystal ball, only this ball had all the countries of the world printed on it. Yesterday it had been Alaska, and she'd imagined snowy wastes, frozen rivers, and gold-panners. Today – she looked carefully – her finger was planted in the middle of the Pacific Ocean, nowhere near any land at all. Of course, explorers would have to spend months at a time on sea voyages. She might be seasick, but she would have to put up with that…

"Did I lend you my new pen-wiper?" Maudie asked. Polly sighed with impatience, pulled back to the school-room, and the prospect of algebra with Miss Dawes.

cs

Lily's departure had taken all the fun out of dawdling home and finding detours, going to see the dairy horses in Old Church Street, or up to the King's Road to look in shop windows, or the long way back along the Embankment to watch the boats going past and sniff the salty air that carried a tang of the sea.

Back at home, Polly took her satchel upstairs, then went straight out to the swing tree in the hope of seeing the new neighbours there. Or maybe they would see her, and come out to finish their "tour"?

But Maurice was there instead, sitting on the swing – *her* swing! – scuffing his feet on the bare earth underneath, and grinning at her. He was in the brown uniform of his school, St. Dunstan's. St. *Dungstan's*, Polly called it, as the boys' blazers were exactly the colour of the heaped, steaming manure left in the road by tradesmen's horses.

"Greetings, Pegs." His grin widened. His red hair was like a thatch, and his face all freckled. *Pegs* was his nickname for her, since he'd seen her initials on her pencil box. She hated being called that. It made her think of clothes pegs, peg legs, square pegs in round holes.

"Hello, Horrible Horace."

Maurice smiled back as if she'd said something nice. It was impossible to offend him.

"Did you know there's a rhyme about walnut trees?" he said, reaching out to touch its bark. "It goes like this: *A dog, a wife and a walnut tree, the more you beat them, the better they be.* My grandad told me."

"That's stupid," Polly retorted. "It's cruel to beat dogs. And why would anyone beat a walnut tree? Only very rough men beat their wives. And why would anyone be better for being beaten? It would only make you bad-tempered and upset."

Maurice grinned again, as if he knew something she didn't. Lazily, he got off the swing. "Come and see what I've found."

She might have guessed it would be something unpleasant. At the farthest end of the garden, where the shrubs grew thickly, he pushed aside the lowest leaves of a hydrangea, and revealed an enormous slug – black and shiny, big as a sausage – in the dampness underneath.

"Urrgh!" Polly couldn't help leaping back. There, he'd made her do it again! – behave just as he wanted. She wasn't usually silly about slugs or other creeping forms of life. After all, she was going to meet all kinds of creatures – slimy or scaly, feathered or furred – when she became an explorer. She'd be very annoyed with herself if she jumped back squealing each time she came across something strange.

"Do you know what it is?" Maurice asked.

"'Course I do. It's a slug, stupid. One of your relations, I expect. Tell the gardener to get rid of it."

"It's not just an *ordinary* slug." Maurice made his eyes round and his voice low and menacing. "It's the very rare Nocturnal Man-Eating Slug, feared by all travellers and explorers. Do you know what they do? They wait till night-time, then they creep across the lawn. They get into houses, creep in through cellar openings and ventilation grilles. There's no way of keeping them out. Then they smell out their victims. They like flesh – that's why they're so enormous. Specially children's flesh – it's not so tough. While you're fast asleep, they come sliming all over you, waiting to feast on flesh—"

"Oh, stop it!" Polly felt the skin on her arms and legs creeping, and only by an effort of will forced herself not to turn and run. "They'll find *you* first then, won't they, on the ground floor? I'd watch out if I were you." She turned to claim the swing. "And be very careful not to sleep with your mouth open," she added over her shoulder.

Reaching the swing, she heard the creak of a window opening above her, and a voice called down. "Polly!"

She stepped back to see past the tree branches and up to the second floor, where Violet Cross was shaking a duster out of the window. "I've got the kettle on," Violet called. "Want to come and see the chaos up here?"

Maurice hadn't followed, and was poking about in the undergrowth, no doubt looking for more man-eating slugs, but she made a point of calling back to him, "Excuse me. I've got someone *interesting* to talk to."

Chapter Five

Cat and Mouse

It was only after Polly had been in the drawing room of the top flat for ten minutes that she remembered to feel sad that it was no longer Lily's. It hardly looked the same at all: the familiar furniture had gone, there were new curtains up at the window, and the floor was stacked with boxes, higgledy-piggledy.

"Excuse the mess," Edwina said, indicating the boxes. "We've got so many books, and nowhere to put them, till we get extra shelves put up. But do sit on my new chaise longue. Don't you think it's just beautiful?" She gestured towards the seat that seemed to take pride of place, upholstered in green velvet and with a scrolled back and armrest.

"As if we haven't got enough bits and pieces, she has to go buying more!" Violet said, rolling her eyes upward.

"It was in the window of Hauptmann's, in the King's Road. I just couldn't resist treating myself to it," Edwina explained. "I've always wanted one, and thought I deserved a coming-out-of-prison present. You can test it for comfort, Polly."

Polly settled herself on the chaise longue while Edwina perched on a crate and Violet settled on the windowsill to wait for the tea to brew. It was all so different from Polly's mother's way of inviting people to tea. Mama would never dream of shouting to someone from a window, nor of inviting them in on the spur of the moment. Invitations to tea were always made in advance, and Mrs. Parks would bake a cake and prepare bread and butter, or thin sandwiches with the crusts cut off.

And Mama would never contemplate letting anyone through the door if the flat was untidy – not that it ever was, with Mrs. Parks in charge. Here the tea was in mugs, and biscuits were eaten straight from the tin. Besides Violet and Edwina, there was a pretty, pert-faced girl of about eighteen, introduced as "Kitty, who looks after us", and who must be the maid, but it was Violet who poured the tea and handed it round.

"Just imagine!" cried Edwina, who seemed full of energy this afternoon, not tired at all. "This whole house once belonged to one family! Your flat, Polly, *and* the one on the ground floor, *and* this one, *and* the servants' bedrooms in the attic – how splendidly people used to live!"

"*Some* people," Violet corrected.

"Well, of course that's what I meant."

"If you go into the Dalbys' flat, on the ground floor,

you can see how it used to be," Polly said, finding herself less shy than she had expected; the others listened to her, smiling and attentive, just as if she were someone their own age. "That's the one my mother would really like to live in. It's got black and white tiles in the hall, made of marble, and an archway that leads to the stairs – and then the big wide staircase that doesn't lead anywhere! It goes halfway up, turns the corner, then heads straight for a wall – the wall and the extra bit of floor that were put in when the house was split into flats. But you can see what a grand house it used to be, when you could walk straight on up. Then, it was only the servants that used our back stairs. Mrs. Parks told me."

"I'd love to have seen it!" said Edwina.

She could easily have been the lady of the house, Polly thought. Her fair hair was swept back from her face and pinned up neatly; with her straight nose and sharp chin she looked as well-bred as a greyhound or a racehorse; her clothes – a dark skirt, and high-

collared cream blouse with embroidered panels –
looked expensive and well made. She had the sort of
voice that could easily be used for ordering servants
about, or for complaining that the knives and forks
weren't polished highly enough. Violet, with her
blouse coming untucked from her skirt, and the toes
of her shoes scuffed, looked more like the person who
did the polishing, or took the orders. Polly still hadn't
decided whether Violet, as well as Kitty, worked for
Edwina in some way. It was hard to tell in such a
strange set-up. None of the other grown-ups Polly
knew would have dreamed of introducing the maid,
just as if she were their equal.

"Lend a hand folding pamphlets, Poll?" Violet,
having handed round the sugar bowl and the one
spoon that could be found, and taken one of the mugs
to Kitty in the kitchen, now carried yet another box
into the room. "We're holding a meeting here tonight,
and I've only just picked these up from the printer's
on my way home from work."

"Work?" Polly echoed, remembering Mrs. Dalby's questions.

Violet glanced at her. "That's right. I work in the WSPU office. Women's Social and Political Union. Typewriting, filing, bit of accounting. I love it!"

Real work, Polly thought – just like Papa, who went off to the bank every morning and did important things there. What would Mrs. Dalby make of that, Polly wondered? Ladies didn't work, so that must mean Violet wasn't a lady, whereas Edwina clearly was. But Violet sounded as if she'd *choose* to work, even if she didn't have to.

"We'll be needing these for the meeting." Edwina ripped open the box. "We're planning a march to the Town Hall, in a fortnight's time. The Lord Mayor and the councillors are holding a special evening reception there, and a banquet. It's going to turn out much more exciting than they think!"

"So you'll both be marching?" Polly asked, remembering yesterday's difference of opinion.

"Well, yes – but Edwina's plan is to get re-arrested and taken back to Holloway," said Violet, stacking sheets of paper in piles. "That's if she manages to stay out of prison till then," she added, with one of the meaningful looks at her friend that Polly took as a sign that they'd argued about this.

"Why? What are you going to do?" Polly imagined Edwina throwing bricks at the Town Hall windows, or attacking the Lord Mayor himself, flying at him like a wildcat as he mounted the steps, resplendent in his robe and chains.

"I won't have to do anything. Just be there. Cat and Mouse, remember," Edwina said, making her hands like claws. "But actually I shall be making a speech."

"She's still officially in Holloway," Violet said, with a wry shake of her head. "Only let out to get her strength back. Soon as the Cats see she's fit enough to go speechifying and waving banners in the King's Road, she'll be locked up again."

"So why go, then?" Polly appealed to Edwina.

"Couldn't you just stay here, out of sight? After all, mice don't usually march about in front of cats – they run away behind the skirting boards!"

Violet shook her head. "Wouldn't suit Edwina, being *that* mouse-like. Bit too much tiger about her, if you ask me."

"What would be the point of hiding?" Edwina asked Polly, with one of her steely looks.

"Well!" It seemed so obvious. "So you don't have to go back and be ill again. Just when you're starting to get better."

"Oh, Polly." Violet shook her head. "Edwina *wants* to go back to Holloway. Go on hunger strike again. Die, if need be. It's good publicity, see, for the Cause."

"You don't really want to die, do you?" Polly asked Edwina, in a small, shocked voice.

Edwina laughed. "Not till I've had the chance to vote! No, I know my own strengths and weaknesses well enough. What I've done is nothing, compared to Emmeline and Sylvia. I've only been arrested three times and sentenced twice. Sylvia's been in and out of prison for the last eight years!"

"Didn't realize it was a competition," Violet said lightly. "And where's your other heroine – Christabel? Run away to Paris, sending instructions to the rest of us, saying what we're to do next! Here, Polly. Fold them twice, like this, so they'll fit the envelopes. You fold, I'll stick them in, Edwina can write the addresses."

The people they were talking about – Emmeline, Sylvia and Christabel – were, Polly knew, the famous Mrs. Pankhurst and her daughters. This was so exciting, she thought – hearing Violet and Edwina talk about people who appeared in the newspapers, and who everyone had heard of! She must tell Lily in her next letter. Edwina cleared a space on a cluttered table and found a pen, while Polly looked at the folded leaflet Violet had given her.

THE CAT AND MOUSE ACT
MUST NOT DETER US FROM
MAKING OUR VIEWS KNOWN!

JOIN the **WSPU** PROTEST MARCH
to the CHELSEA TOWN HALL to
CONFRONT the LORD MAYOR
and COUNCILLORS

at an IMPORTANT
CIVIC RECEPTION and BANQUET.

ASSEMBLE at SPEAKER'S CORNER,
HYDE PARK,
5 pm, SATURDAY 11th JULY.

BRING BANNERS, WEAR **WSPU** COLOURS.

WOMEN'S SOCIAL
&
POLITICAL UNION

Immediately, Polly wanted to go too, but she couldn't help remarking, "Not all women want the vote, though, do they? Mama, and Mrs. Dalby, and Great Aunt Millicent – *they* don't. I've heard them talking about it."

"What do they say?" said Edwina, with her head down, writing.

Polly tried to remember. "Things like – *Leave it to the men. No need for us to trouble our heads.* That sort of thing."

Edwina looked up, amused; she made a snorting noise, just like the milkman's horse. "*Leave it to the men?* Yes, and see where that's got us! Strikes, the Irish Question, dreadful conditions in factories, desperate poverty in the East End – that's how good the politicians are at sorting things out!"

Polly didn't know much about any of these things. "I'm only saying what –"

"Yes, I know – but what your aunt and mother say, that's a way of not having to think for themselves! Shouldn't women have a say in who represents us in Parliament? Shouldn't we be entitled to put our views?"

"All right, Edie, you're not on your soapbox now," Violet said calmly. "No need to start yelling. Polly can hear you all right."

Edwina stopped in mid-breath, and smiled apologetically at Polly. "Sorry. Sorry. I get carried away. But it's quite true, you know! When you grow up, Polly, unless the government sees sense, you won't be entitled to vote, won't have a say in the running of the country – no matter how sensible, how accomplished, how capable or thoughtful you are. Whereas – think of the most thuggish, nasty boy you know –"

"Maurice," Polly said, without hesitation.

"Maurice? All right – or, say, someone who grows up to be a drunkard, who gambles away his money, who beats his wife and ill-treats his children – *he'll* be entitled to vote, but you won't. Does that seem fair to you?"

"No!" said Polly hotly. "Of course it isn't!"

Violet licked and sealed an envelope. "She won't stop till you're a signed-up member of the WSPU, Polly, you realize that?"

"Well, it's important!" Edwina said. "We need a new generation of women to come along and take over when we've exhausted ourselves –"

"– when you've starved yourself to death, you mean. Have another biscuit."

"The thing is, Polly, you can make up your own mind." Edwina took a Bourbon cream with one hand and reached for an envelope with the other. "You don't have to let anyone else tell you what to think. Not even me."

Polly was struck by a new thought. "Our new baby – my baby brother, assuming he's a boy, which everyone seems to think – when he grows up, he'll be able to vote, even though he's not even born yet, and I won't, even though I'm older!" She looked from Edwina's face to Violet's. "That's *definitely* not right, is it?"

"No, it's not," said Violet.

Edwina smiled at her. "There, you see – you're thinking for yourself. Seeing how things are. Wondering if things ought to change. Are you any good at sewing, Polly?"

"Sewing?" Polly echoed. Sewing was exactly the sort

of thing Mama approved of – a long way from protesting in the streets!

"Banners." Edwina nodded towards a bulging package under the table. "All that fabric's got to be turned into banners. Purple, white and green, with lettering. Will you help us?"

Polly wasn't much good at sewing – "all fingers and thumbs" Miss Thripp called her at school; Lily was the one who was neat and deft with a needle. But she answered without hesitation. "Yes. Yes, of course I will."

Chapter Six

Secret Suffragette

In the early hours of Monday morning, Polly lay in bed, hot, restless and worrying.

She *had* been asleep, but now, at half past two in the morning (she had crept out to the hall, to check by the grandfather clock) she felt wider awake than ever. With the new electric lights, she could easily have turned on her lamp to read, but felt certain she wouldn't be able to concentrate. She had pushed back the sheets, blanket and quilt, but still felt hot and fidgety.

She was hungry, too, and that wasn't a very good beginning to the day, as she had decided not to eat anything at all for twenty-four hours. If Edwina could go without food for nearly a week, Polly wanted to prove to herself that she could manage just one day. Now that she was a suffragette, or suffragist, she would have to be willing to put herself to the test. She hadn't told anyone she was a suffragette; but how could she not be, now that it had been explained to her? It was so obviously unreasonable for things to continue as they were. If she felt herself wavering, Polly had only to think of Maurice, and his smug, superior smile. Why should he think himself more important than her, just because he happened to be a boy?

What was keeping her awake was the problem of what Mama would say when she found out that Violet and Edwina were suffragettes, as she must surely discover when Edwina came to tea tomorrow – no, today. It would have to be Edwina on her own, since Violet would be at work. Suffragettes, to Mama, were a strange new breed of savage women, with their weapons and their firebombs, their angry voices and their fierce determination.

"What must their husbands think?" Polly had heard her remark to Meredith Dalby. "Their families? How can they bear to demean themselves by shouting in the streets?"

Polly couldn't imagine Mama shouting in the street, not even if there were a burglary, or a fire! To Mama, *decorum* was the rule for female behaviour. "A little more decorum, please, girls!" she would say, if Polly and Lily laughed too uproariously over a silly game, or rushed downstairs to feed lump sugar to the rag-and-bone man's horse. *Decorum* meant always being polite, always being mild and quiet and ladylike, never making a stir. *Boys* didn't have to worry about decorum. Maurice and the other St. Dunstan's boys were allowed to shout, to kick footballs, to have rough play-fights. It wasn't that Polly actually wanted to do those things; it just seemed unfair that boys could do so much more.

"You know," Polly had remarked to Lily once, "I really wish *I'd* been a boy!"

"Well, *I* don't," Lily retorted. "Imagine not being able to wear nice clothes or hair ribbons, or have pretty things! You mean you'd rather be Maurice?"

"Well, no, not *Maurice* –"

"And you can't do anything about it, so what's the point of wishing?" Lily had pointed out.

Polly couldn't help thinking, sometimes, that Lily was exactly the sort of daughter Mama wanted – pretty and neat, always polite and respectful. Lily's fair hair, of which she was very proud, was always brushed and shining, not plain, dull brown like Polly's. Now Mama had invited into her drawing room a young woman who cared nothing for decorum, who had attacked a policeman outside Buckingham Palace, and had been a prisoner at Holloway! It would almost be funny, if

Polly didn't care so much about being friends with Edwina and Violet. Because they did seem to be her friends, surprising though it was; they had actually said so. They had far more important things to bother about, yet they bothered with *her*.

She had to prove herself worthy of them by persisting with her hunger strike.

At breakfast time, still yawning after her broken night, she said that she didn't want any of the porridge Mrs. Parks was preparing in the kitchen. The sideboard was set temptingly with pots of jam and honey, and the salty smell of Papa's breakfast kippers lingered, but Polly made herself say, "I don't want any porridge, thank you, Mrs. Parks. I'm not hungry."

Mama heard, of course. She was getting so big now, with the baby inside her, that she could only just fit between the dining table and the sideboard. "Oh, Polly! Are you feeling queasy? Dizzy? I do hope you're not going down with something." She placed a cool hand on Polly's forehead. "You don't feel as if you're running a temperature – but perhaps you ought to stay at home today, just in case. Shall I call Dr. Mayes?"

"No! No, I'm quite all right really," Polly said hastily. Hunger striking would be even harder if she had to spend the day in bed, with nothing to do but think about food. "Just not hungry, that's all."

By lunchtime she felt ravenous, and the meat and potatoes served up in the refectory smelled more delicious than anything she could have imagined. She made herself pretend to pick at her food, then offer it to Maudie Marchant, who was always willing to eat up what anyone else didn't want. She managed to slide her portion on to Maudie's plate without any of the teachers noticing. It was harder to resist treacle pudding and custard, but she made herself go without, though her stomach gave a rumble of outrage and her greedy eyes devoured every mouthful taken by the girls at her table. Some of them even had seconds. Really, she ought to get extra credit for that –

the suffragettes in their prison cells didn't have to watch other people gorging on treacle pudding! She sipped at a glass of water, beginning to feel quite virtuous. If anyone asked why she wasn't eating, she could say she was excited about the summer holidays beginning this week.

The walk home seemed twice as long as usual. On the corner of Pimlico Road, the news vendor's billboard said that an Austrian Archduke had been shot dead in Sarajevo. It sounded rather exciting.

"Where's Sarah-jeevo?" Polly asked the vendor, balancing on one leg while she removed a stone from her shoe.

The man shrugged. "Balkans, it says, Miss. Never heard of it neever." A pin-striped man, about to walk briskly past, glanced at the board and stopped, handing over a coin. Polly retied her shoelace and trudged on home.

Her legs ached wearily as she climbed the stairs. Mrs. Parks was scuttling out of the kitchen, carrying a tray loaded with the best tea set. There were voices in the drawing room, and Mrs. Dalby's tinkling laughter.

Preoccupied with her hollow stomach, Polly had almost forgotten – it was the tea party she had been fearing! She went into her bedroom to put down her satchel, tidy her hair – the good thing about wearing it in pigtails was that it never really got *un*tidy – and wash her hands for tea. Then, feeling very self-conscious, she went to join the grown-ups. The room was fuller than she had expected – Mrs. Dalby was there, and Edwina, but also Great Aunt Millicent, filling her armchair with a vast puff of frilled organdie, and Great Uncle Victor, thin and moustached, in a tweed suit and a cravat in spite of the heat of the day, sitting to attention with his walking stick propped in front of him, resting both hands on its silver handle. Polly had barely time to glance at Edwina before Great Aunt Millicent cried, "Polly, dear! Come and give your great aunt a kiss! My, my – what a pretty young lady you're turning into!"

Dutifully, Polly kissed them each in turn – Great Aunt Millicent smelling of face powder and freesia perfume, Great Uncle Victor of pipe tobacco and coal-tar soap. "Quite the image of your mother!" her great aunt continued. "And she says you're being *such* a help, in her confinement!"

"Am I?" Polly turned to her mother.

"Darling, of course you are." Mama summoned Polly to stand beside her. "Miss Rutherford, I believe you've met my daughter Polly?"

"Yes, indeed. How do you do, Polly?" said Edwina. She was wearing a dress of aquamarine silk with the fashionable square neckline, her fair hair was sleekly dressed, and she looked quite at home in Mama's elegant drawing room – as decorous as Mama could have wished.

"Very well, thank you." Polly felt shy, as if this were a different Edwina from the one she had met before.

"I'm so sorry, Miss Rutherford," Mama said. "I

interrupted you. You were telling us about your acquaintance with the Earl of Belmont?"

"Oh yes. You see he's a second or third cousin, or something like that. It was through another cousin of mine, Edward Holdsworth – do you know the Holdsworths of Eaton Square? – that I heard the flat was to fall vacant. He and the Belmonts know each other from shooting parties, and I've met them myself at the odd dinner party…"

Polly sat on a stool and listened with amazement as Edwina played the part of the perfect drawing-room guest, giving no hint of the passions that drove her. So fascinating was the impersonation that Polly had accepted and eaten a slice of coffee cake before she remembered her hunger strike. She could imagine Mrs. Dalby – and even her mother – at the haberdashery counter of Peter Jones, remarking loudly, "Our new neighbour's a cousin of the Earl of Belmont – our landlord, don't you know. Yes, we had tea together just the other day."

When Edwina had finished explaining about the flat, Maurice's mother ventured, "What a pity your friend, Miss Cross, wasn't able to join us! Now tell me – I'm not quite clear what her role is. Is she your secretary, maybe?"

Edwina gave a gentle smile. "No – I am not her employer. She is my friend – we share the flat, and work together."

"Oh! At what kind of work?"

"We are campaigners for women's suffrage," said Edwina.

She spoke matter-of-factly, but Polly's eyes darted quickly round the room to take in everyone's reactions. Mama's hostess smile hardly wavered, but Mrs. Dalby shot her a keen, almost triumphant glance, signalling wait-till-we-discuss-this-later. Great Uncle Victor took a sharp breath, and clutched his walking stick more tightly. "Well!" said Great Aunt Millicent, closing her eyes as if needing to assimilate the news in private.

Mrs. Dalby was first to recover. "And what exactly," she asked, silky-smooth, "might this campaigning consist of?"

Chapter Seven

That Sort of Person

Gossip, gossip, gossip! It must be Meredith Dalby's favourite pastime, Polly thought. She couldn't imagine anything more pointless.

When everyone left, at the end of the tea party, Mrs. Dalby wished Edwina a cold "good day", and went downstairs to her own flat, only to return half an hour later. Polly wasn't at all surprised. She guessed the reason: to discuss Edwina with Mama, in private.

The two women settled in the drawing room, side by side on the sofa, and Mama rang the bell to order a fresh pot of tea from Mrs. Parks. They never seemed to tire of drinking tea and talking.

"Well, my dear!" Mrs. Dalby told Mama, with a trophy-hunter's relish. "You'll never guess what I've just found out from my Elsie! She's been talking to their maid, and *she* said –"

Polly was supposed to be practising the piano, but with Mrs. Dalby and Mama in firm occupation of the drawing room, she had the perfect excuse for slacking. The door was ajar; as soon as Mrs. Parks had taken in the tea, Polly stood just outside, anxious not to miss a single word of Mrs. Dalby's revelations.

"Holloway Prison…violent conduct in the street, attacking a policeman, if you can believe it!" Mrs. Dalby went on, in shocked delight.

"Meredith! No!"

"It's true, I assure you! Only out on licence…may well end up back there…yes, really, my dear!… A meeting there the other night…posters and leaflets everywhere, a sort of headquarters…well, who knows? Weapons, a bomb factory? You know some of these women will stop at nothing, they're quite fanatical… What if the police raid the premises?… She's been completely disowned by her parents, Elsie told me… they're related to the Rutherfords at Kew…and I can't say I'm the slightest bit surprised… Yes, com*pletely* unsuitable…and enticing Polly up there!"

A startled sound from Mama: Polly shrank back, though her ears strained for what Mrs. Dalby said next.

"Oh yes! Maurice told me. He was with Polly in the garden, when one of them called to her from the window and invited her in, and of course – such a docile little thing she is! – she trotted straight up there."

Polly felt herself going hot all over. *Docile little thing!* She wasn't entirely sure what *docile* meant, but would find out later. As for Maurice – what a tattle-tale, running straight to his mother to tell on her! She'd have something to say to him tomorrow –

But Mrs. Dalby hadn't finished yet. "My dear, you must put your foot down very firmly! I can't get over the nerve of her, Miss Airs and Graces, sitting there as if butter wouldn't melt in her mouth, going on about the Earl of Belmont! I should think he'd disown her too, if he had the slightest inkling what she's up to! I shall write to him personally…it's quite disgraceful, so inconsiderate to the rest of us… And the other one, who I'm not surprised didn't even show her face, is from the East End. From *Bethnal Green*, my dear! No doubt thinks herself a very clever little minx, wheedling herself into the favours of Her Ladyship up there…"

Polly listened, appalled, barely recognizing Violet and Edwina from these caricatures. Mama, hardly able to get a word in, made occasional murmurs of assent or outrage.

At last there were sounds of Mrs. Dalby rising to

her feet, preparing to leave; quickly Polly scuttled to her bedroom, almost bumping into Mrs. Parks, who said nothing but wagged a finger at her, knowing she'd been eavesdropping.

As soon as the door closed behind Mrs. Dalby, Polly confronted her mother.

"Mama! She came back to tell you things about Edw – about Miss Rutherford," she corrected herself. "Didn't she? I know she doesn't like them – but you can't believe everything she says! You know it's only gossip!"

Mama put a hand to her back. "But how *much* of it is gossip? You know the saying – there's no smoke without fire. Is it true that you went up to Flat Three, and didn't see fit to tell me about it?"

Polly was silent; Mama gave her a reproachful look. "I'm afraid, darling, it looks as if you haven't been very truthful. Have you? I really don't want you to come into contact with that sort of person. *Most* unfortunate that they live in the same building. Yes, it was I who invited Miss Rutherford here – but that was before I knew."

"Well," Polly retorted, "I *like* That Sort of Person – far better than I like Mrs. Dalby's Sort of Person. All she does is—"

"*Polly!*" her mother said sharply. "I will not have you speak to me like that, nor show such disrespect to Mrs. Dalby!"

"Sorry," Polly mumbled. But it was true. She did like Violet and Edwina far more than she liked Maurice's mother, even though she'd only just met them. Edwina and Violet were *interesting*! They thought differently from other people. They cared nothing for decorum or what was expected of them. She tried again. "They're my friends! I like them! You're not going to stop me being friends with them, are you?"

"Friends? Now you're just being ridiculous," Mama said sharply. "You've only known them a matter of days. Do you think women like those are likely to be interested in someone your age, a schoolgirl?"

But they *are*, Polly thought mutinously. They *are* interested in me, and not only because I've promised to help them. Nothing could have been more flattering than to be asked. There could be no question of going back on her word.

"We'll wait and see what your father has to say," Mama said firmly. "Now I really must rest, and I suggest you do your piano practice. You've been skimping it lately, haven't you?"

Wait-and-see-what-your-father-has-to-say was usually a bad sign. When he came home from the bank just after six, he and Mama retired to the drawing room with their before-dinner sherry – this time with the door firmly closed. By the time they came out, Papa had made a New Rule.

"Polly, I have told your mother that I will not have you consorting with those women upstairs. If you meet them coming in or out, you may nod, and wish them a polite 'good morning', or 'good afternoon'; but that is all."

"But—"

"Don't answer me back, young lady! I have made a Rule, and I expect you to follow it. If your mother had had any idea what this Miss Rutherford is really like, she would never have considered inviting her into our home. I'm very shocked to hear you've been up to their flat without permission – don't let me hear of such a thing again."

At dinner Polly gazed gloomily at her plate. She wasn't hungry; she might as well have gone all day without eating, after all.

"Don't pick at your food, Polly," her mother reproved. "And sit up straight. If you can't be cheerful, at least remember your table manners."

Do this, don't do that. Be a good girl. Do as you're told. Sometimes it seemed this was all she ever heard.

What now? She couldn't let down Edwina and Violet, after promising to help them; couldn't simply say *my parents won't let me.* Not to someone who'd rather go to prison than do as she was told!

Don't let me hear of such a thing again…those were Papa's precise words.

Don't let me hear…

The more his phrase echoed in her head, the more it seemed to offer another meaning. Funny, Polly thought, how you could bend words when you tried. Do it, but don't let Papa find out. All right then! Since that was what he wanted…

After dinner she remembered to look up *docile* in Papa's big dictionary.

Easily led or taught, it said; *obedient*.

Puh! went Polly. She slammed the heavy dictionary shut. Obedient? Easily led? We'll see about *that*.

Chapter Eight

Dog at Heel

For years and years, ever since Polly had started at The Mary Burnet School, she and Lily had been escorted to and fro: at first by their nanny, later by one or other of the mothers. Only for the last year and a half had they been allowed to go unaccompanied. Officially, now that Lily was gone, Polly was supposed to walk to school and back with Maurice, but she usually tried to avoid him. This was easy to do, as the way in and out of the first- and second-floor flats was from Flood Street at the side. Only the Dalbys' ground-floor flat had the grand Chelsea Walk entrance, through the iron gates and up the steps to the massive front door. Mama sighed with envy over Flat Number One's splendour, but Polly preferred being on the first floor, at tree-height, even if it meant going in and out the side way.

Although she tried to give Maurice the slip, he sometimes lurked in wait for her. On Tuesday morning, in Royal Hospital Road, he ran up behind her and tugged at one of her pigtails.

"You'd better watch it, Pegs, being friends with jailbirds! It might be infectious!" He was still panting from the run to catch her up.

"Better stay away from me, then," Polly said crossly, straightening her straw boater. "Anyway, that's all *you* know."

"It's true! My mother said!"

"Your mother doesn't know everything. She makes

half of it up if you ask me, just to have something to gossip about." Dodging round a dairy cart, Polly crossed to the other side of the road, but Maurice trotted behind her like a spaniel at heel. She rounded on him, remembering. "And what she doesn't know, *you* tell her! Why are you such a beastly tell-tale? Had you run out of slugs and toads to play with?"

Maurice stared at her open-mouthed. "Well, I didn't know it was telling tales! How was I to know you weren't supposed—"

"Aren't you a bit old to be telling your mother everything?" Polly was in no mood to listen. "Does she have to tell you what to think? Mind your own business, next time! And your Elsie's just as bad, spreading rumours—"

"It's *all* of our business, my mother says – we live in the same house. All the same," Maurice said, kicking a stone along the gutter, "it's a lot more interesting than your friend lily-white, living with jailbirds!"

"I wish Lily could have stayed, and *you'd* moved

out!" Polly marched on, hoping to shake Maurice off, especially when she saw two other boys in dung-brown blazers standing by the entrance to the Royal Hospital Gardens.

"I wonder if they'll –" he began, still at her shoulder, keeping pace.

She surprised him into silence by turning abruptly to face him. "Good dog, Maurice! *Here*, boy!" she called, loudly enough for the other boys to hear. "Sit! *Good* boy!"

"Oh, what're –"

The two boys had heard, just as she planned, and now Maurice was the centre of attention. "*Ruff! Ruff!*" barked the taller boy, while the other held up his hands like paws, and lolled his tongue out, panting. Maurice's face turned bright red, clashing horribly with his ginger hair.

Ha! Served him right. Abandoning him to their taunts, Polly marched on towards Norton Terrace.

 C3

By the end of the afternoon, turning into Wellington Square for her music lesson with Mrs. Langrish, Polly couldn't help but feel optimistic. It was the vacation – weeks and weeks of it stretched ahead, day after long summer day. And, in August, a seaside holiday in Folkestone; that would be fun. Meanwhile, at home, no one could watch her every minute of the day, and it wasn't as if she had to escape from the house to see Violet and Edwina – only tiptoe up the stairs, or talk to them in the garden.

Polly thought of Mrs. Langrish as Aunt Dorothy, even though she was Lily's aunt, not hers. She lived in one of the elegant white houses that lined Wellington Square, off the King's Road. She was waiting on the doorstep, waving a folded sheet of notepaper.

"Polly! I saw you coming down the Square. Such wonderful news!"

Polly had always liked Lily's aunt. A widow with no children of her own, she doted on her niece, and loved planning picnics, outings and surprise treats. She was small, lively and round-faced – probably older than Mama, with little lines around her eyes, but she was so full of enthusiasm that you could easily think she was younger. "Look! This letter came this morning!" She flourished it gaily. "Dear Lily's coming to stay, in a fortnight, for a whole week! Isn't that marvellous – I know you must be missing her even more than I am. You can read what she says before we start our lesson."

Aunt Dorothy wasn't nearly as strict a piano teacher as Polly's parents liked to imagine, and only scolded Polly very mildly for her lack of practice when she blundered through the mazurka she was supposed to have learned. "We'll try again next week, and you can practise every day in the meantime. Lily will have been doing even less, if I know her. We're going to have such fun when she comes to stay!"

An hour later, arriving home, Polly found a letter awaiting her, from Lily, with the same news.

"That will cheer you up!" said Mama, who was obviously trying to pretend that yesterday hadn't happened. *It'll put that suffragette nonsense out of your head!* she was quite obviously thinking, as clearly as if a caption had unscrolled itself in the air above her.

Polly's view was different. Lily would be her ally, and it would be just as if she had never gone away. Polly might have to do a bit of persuading, but she and Lily always did things together, whenever they could. With Lily staying, there would be all sorts of excuses for outings and picnics. Hyde Park was the obvious place for a picnic, wasn't it? And maybe Polly would just happen to discover that she had a banner packed with her sandwiches instead of a napkin: a banner of purple, white and green.

Chapter Nine

Quarrel

"I've come to help with the banners," Polly said, at the door to Flat Three.

It was Edwina who had answered her ring. "Hello, Polly! Good of you to come back so soon." She didn't seem at all surprised; but then she didn't know what a dreadful gossip Mrs. Dalby was, or how indiscreet Kitty had been. In the drawing room, she pulled out a large fabric-stuffed bag from behind an armchair.

"Violet's in charge of this really, but I know she's cut out some letters ready. Here are some of the banners, already sewn together." She pulled out a broad band, made from long strips of purple and green. "The letters are white, you see – they'll spell out VOTES FOR WOMEN, and WE DEMAND THE RIGHT TO VOTE. You'd better pin the letters on first, to get the spacing right. Here's Violet's sewing box" – she flipped open the lid – "with everything you need. Will you excuse me while I finish this article? I must get it in the post for tomorrow. Then I'll sew with you."

"I can't stay long." Polly glanced at the clock on the mantelpiece. "Mama has a lie-down this time of day, and –" She stopped, not wanting to say that she was forbidden to be here. Edwina glanced at her, and she said instead: "Such good news – Lily's coming to stay, in two weeks! My best friend Lily, whose flat this used to be."

"How lovely! I shall invite you both to tea," Edwina said at once. "I'll ask Kitty to bake a special cake."

"It's very kind of you," Polly said formally; but her brain was churning over the new problem this created. How could she bring Lily to tea, when she wasn't allowed here herself? And in any case, wouldn't Lily hate to see her flat, her own bedroom, all changed and cluttered with other people's things? And what would Edwina think of Lily, with her good-girl manners and her love of pretty things?

"That's settled, then. I shall look forward to it!" Edwina moved to the writing desk in the corner, which was arranged like a small office, with an upright chair, typewriter, and stacks of box files and papers.

While Polly sorted out fabric letters and pinned them to the banner, Edwina bashed the keys at furious speed, occasionally breaking off with a "Blast!" when she made a mistake. (Mama would be shocked about that, too – a lady, cursing like a workman!) Fascinated, Polly kept glancing at her. Perhaps Edwina earned money by working at home, doing people's typing for them? A record was playing from a gramophone on the floor, the music punctuated by the uneven clatter of keys, the ting of the bell at the end of each line, and the swoosh as Edwina tugged back the carriage.

"There!" Edwina said at last, pulling out her final sheet of paper.

"Is this what you do?" Polly looked up from threading a needle. "Secretary work?"

"No, it's journalism. I write articles for various newspapers. It's a way of spreading the word, you see. I take every opportunity I can."

"Oh!" Polly felt out of her depth. Writing for newspapers! It sounded very impressive: maybe Edwina wrote pieces in *The Times* newspaper Papa read every day! But if they were about votes for women, he wouldn't read them – just huff, and turn to the business pages.

"What do you want to do when you leave school, Polly?" Edwina said, rummaging in the bureau drawers.

Polly hesitated; then said in a rush, "I want to be an

explorer. I know it's silly, and Mama says girls can't be explorers—"

"Of course they can," Edwina said sharply. "What about Mary Kingsley? What about Gertrude Bell? Women have travelled through Mesopotamia, climbed mountains in the Himalayas. Can't be explorers? Try telling *them* what they can and can't do!"

"Mama and Papa want to send me to Switzerland, to a finishing school. Doesn't it sound funny, being *finished*? It means learning all about manners, and how to give dinner parties, and what to say when you meet a duke or a countess."

"I know. My parents would have sent me to one, but I refused to go. Schools for young ladies!" Edwina gave her horse-like *hrrrumph*. "Finished! Finished as an independent human being, more like! Education, that's what girls need. Exactly the same education as boys. The same opportunities. If you want to be an explorer, Polly, that's what you should be. Where do you want to go?"

"Oh –" Polly thought of all the countries in the atlas and on the globe, the places her finger had landed. "Africa. Antarctica. India. Australia. Little islands right out in the Pacific Ocean. It's just that – when you look at the world, and see what a small place England is, it seems silly to stay here all your life, just because you happen to be born here, when there are all these other, different places!"

"You're absolutely right there. I must lend you a favourite book of mine – you'll love it, I'm sure. Just a moment –" Edwina left the room, but kept calling out questions from along the hallway: "What's your favourite lesson at school, Polly? What are you good at? What don't you like? Have you got good teachers?"

At first Polly called back her answers: "Geography. I'm best at that, and at Art, and I quite like Games, except in winter. I'm hopeless at Maths and French. I can never remember how irregular French verbs go, and Mam'selle gets so impatient –" After a few minutes of this, as Edwina showed no sign of coming back, Polly followed her.

"Here it is! Knew it was here somewhere." Edwina emerged from one of the bedrooms, holding out a book in a red cover. Polly looked, and read: *Under Desert Skies: the Journal of a Female Traveller*, by Olive Kingston.

"Take it. Borrow it. And anything else you like the look of," Edwina said, brushing dust off her hands.

"Can I?" Polly flicked through the pages, handling the book carefully. "Thank you!" She looked up, and past Edwina at shelves and shelves of books that took up a whole wall of the bedroom. This used to be Lily's room, and there had been only one small shelf above the bed; Edwina must have had these put up specially. "Are they all yours?"

"Have a look." Edwina waved an airy hand. "Borrow as many as you like. I've just got to write a quick letter, then we'll both get on with the sewing."

"I've just remembered something," Polly said. "About the girl who used to live here – the one who planted the walnut tree. She wanted to be a gardener, and people told her it wasn't a job for a girl, but now she is one. Was, rather, because she's old now, and retired. But she worked as Head Gardener at a big house in Sussex. Mrs. Parks told me, because Miss Frazer – I think that was her name – called to see the house, and her walnut tree, when she came to the Flower Show at the Royal Hospital last year."

Edwina looked delighted. "Well, there you are! A wonderful example here in this very house."

She returned to her typing. Polly knew she should be going back downstairs, but couldn't resist; she went into the bedroom and moved along the shelves, touching the spines of books, reading the titles. It was like a private library! Poetry; novels; history; lots of books about politics and the rights of women. No wonder Edwina was so clever, if she'd read all these…

She was looking at *The Mill on the Floss* when she heard a key turn in the lock, and someone entered in a hurry. Violet, it must be. Polly was replacing the book, about to go into the hallway and say hello, when Violet's angry voice made her jump.

"Edwina, I thought you'd promised! A fool, I am, to believe what you say – I *thought* I heard the door, in the middle of the night! Agnes told me – you went sneaking out to break windows, didn't you? It's lucky you're still here, not in Holloway Prison! Only I suppose that's what you want, really?"

Edwina answered, with perfect calmness: "We've got to keep up the pressure. I can't bear to sit about doing nothing."

Violet had marched into the drawing room, but her voice was loud and clear. "It's like a sport to you, though, en't it? Breaking windows under the noses of the police. You're addicted to it!"

"Nonsense!"

"And you haven't got your strength back, not yet," Violet persisted. "Will you promise me – and I mean really promise this time – not to go out again at night?"

"I'll promise nothing of the sort." Edwina sounded

haughty now. "Could you stop shouting, please? You're giving me a headache – and Polly's here."

This was Polly's cue to slink back and join them, red-faced and embarrassed to find herself overhearing such a quarrel.

"Oh, hello, Polly," said Violet, attempting a smile; but then she rounded on Edwina again, evidently too full of outrage to hold it in. "When it comes down to it, it's votes for ladies you're fighting for, en't it? For upper-class ladies. For you and your sort. Not votes for the ordinary working women where I come from – the East Enders, the factory workers, the wives struggling to make ends meet, with five kids and a drunken husband – the ones we really need. How are they meant to make themselves heard?"

Edwina looked at her exasperatedly. "We've got to be single-minded, don't you see that? We can't get sidetracked into all sorts of other causes."

"It's got to be for *every*one, not some sort of – of personal triumph!" Violet stomped over to the window, and stood for a moment leaning on the sill, while Polly looked anxiously from her to Edwina and back again; Edwina, quite composed, addressed an envelope and stuck on a stamp. Kitty came in, raised her eyebrows, then, catching Polly's glance, gave a conspiratorial half-grin, as if she were quite used to spats like these.

"Oh, Kitty," said Edwina, "are you making tea?"

"Nearly ready," Kitty replied; "crumpets, too, if you want."

"Ooh, I should think so. Do we?" Edwina looked at Polly, then at Violet.

Violet wasn't going to be sidetracked by crumpets. "You know, I sometimes wonder if we're fighting for the same thing at all! Sometimes I wonder how much you understand. That chaise long-ew you bought on a whim the other day – that'd be six months' housekeeping for my mum!"

"*Chaise longue*," Edwina corrected, in an emphatically French accent.

Violet looked exasperated. "Oh, Edie, you're such a terrible snob!"

Polly held her breath: how could Violet *say* such things? But, to her amazement, Edwina burst out laughing.

"Yes, you're quite right! Just listen to me! How terribly prissy I am! Let's have tea and crumpets and forget all about our differences."

Violet began to laugh too, and Kitty rolled her eyes at the ceiling and turned for the kitchen.

"Sorry, Polly. You must think we're a pair of alley cats, spitting and scratching!" said Violet, settling herself on the despised chaise longue. "We're not always like this, fortunately. Oh, you've made a start on the sewing!" she added, noticing Polly's work – a V and an O tacked, none too neatly, to a strip of purple and green.

"Yes. But I think I'd better go home now," Polly said awkwardly.

"What, and miss the crumpets? Not because of my

little temper tantrum, I hope?" Violet pulled a rueful face.

"No – it's just that I'm expected."

"Thank you, Polly," said Edwina from her desk. "We're very grateful."

It was Violet who went with her to the door. "Do come again – whenever you like!" she called, as Polly crept down the stairs.

Polly hoped she hadn't spoken loudly enough for Mama to hear. She slid through the front door of Flat Two, which she had left on the latch.

She felt shocked by the vehemence of the argument – almost shaking. Edwina and Violet were behaving now as if nothing had happened; but how could they disagree so strongly, and still be friends?

Chapter Ten

Reasons

Next morning, Polly let herself out into the garden before anyone else was up, even before Mrs. Parks had arrived in the kitchen. She liked to be outside in the early morning: she liked the damp smell of grass and earth, the sense of everything waking up to the day, a wood pigeon cooing in the top of the walnut tree, and the sounds of hooves and wheels in Oakley Street beyond the old mews, which gave her the smug feeling of having a day of leisure ahead of her while the rest of London busied itself with shops and offices and delivery rounds.

She glanced up at the top flat. Perhaps the quarrel last night hadn't been as bad as she thought it at the time. Violet's outburst might be better than the way Papa and Mama went about it, on the rare occasions when they disagreed – not so much an exchange of views as a cooling of the air that spread chillily through the whole flat, so that Polly felt numbed by it.

With her special notebook, Lily's leaving present, she sat on the swing. The seat was wet with dew; immediately she felt dampness through her skirt and petticoats, but it was too late to worry about that now.

Lily's notebook had marbled covers and a silk ribbon bookmark. At first Polly had thought she might write a story in it; but as no story had come to her, she now decided to use it for Plans and Ideas. It would have to be kept secret, of course; she would hide it under her pillow, wrapped in her nightdress.

Plans and Ideas, she wrote carefully on the first page. *Find out about being an explorer. Read "Under Desert Skies" and lots of other books.* Then, on page two, a heading: *Ten Reasons why Maurice shouldn't have the vote.*

She sucked the end of her pencil, then went on:

1. *He tells tales.*
2. *He is rude.*
3. *He treads on ants.*
4. *He pulls girls' hair and knocks their hats off in the street.*
5. *He took the last jam tart at teatime without asking if anyone else wanted it.*
6. *He thinks he knows everything.*
7. *He stole Lily's doll and threw her up in the tree and laughed when she got caught by her hair.*
8. *He is a horrible, slimy, nasty, unkind boy.*

9. *He thinks boys are better than girls.*
10. *He will be even worse by the time he is grown-up and old enough to vote.*

There! she thought with satisfaction, drawing a squiggly line underneath. That was Maurice summed up!

"Morning, Polly!"

It was Violet, coming out from the back-stairs entrance with a basket of laundry under her arm, making for the washing line at the end of the garden, which was separated from the lawn by a bed of shrubs.

Polly darted across. "Let me help!"

"You're out early – what a glorious day!" Violet propped the heavy basket against one hip. "Just putting these out before I go off to work." She looked so cheerful that Polly could hardly believe she was the same person who'd ranted at Edwina last night. She couldn't decide which of the two young women she liked best: Violet, for her kindness and ordinariness, or Edwina, so clever and determined. Just imagine, going out on a window-smashing raid, after a demure tea with Mama and Mrs. Dalby!

According to Papa, Polly should have said a stiff "good morning", and gone straight indoors.

"I'm not supposed to talk to you," she confided. "And now Edwina says she'll invite me and Lily to tea – that's my best friend Lily who used to live in your flat. Only we won't be allowed!"

"Oh?"

"It's Papa, you see. He's terribly strict." Polly explained about Papa's New Rule, while they pegged out the blouses and undergarments (she could just imagine Mrs. Dalby having something to say about *that*, if she ventured this far down the garden: "How utterly shameless! Underclothes hanging on a washing line, for the whole world to see! Did you ever hear the like?")

Violet listened in concern, then said, "I wouldn't want to stir up trouble for you, with your ma and pa. Shame though – just when we was getting to know one another! Can't you talk to your pa – convince him we're really quite human?"

"I don't know," Polly said doubtfully. Papa was not really open to negotiation, once he'd made his views known.

"Anyway, that's a job done. Thank you," said Violet, when the washing was pegged jauntily on the line. "We'll find a way, somehow or other. You can always blame it on me if your pa finds out."

"But I want to carry on helping with the banners and leaflets!" They were walking slowly back up the garden.

"Well, you know you're always welcome – whenever you can come up for the odd half hour. You know the old saying, *What the eye doesn't see, the heart doesn't grieve over*?"

Polly considered. That did sound rather like her own thinking; but it hadn't stopped Violet from being angry when Edwina slipped out of their flat without telling her. It sounded fine as a saying, but she wasn't sure how well it would work.

Violet paused, seeing the notebook on the swing seat where Polly had left it. "That yours? Are you writing a story?"

"No, not a story." Polly fetched it. "Here. I did this." She handed over the open book and stood self-consciously while Violet read the list, sure now that it was a very childish thing to have done.

Violet laughed. "Poor Maurice! You can't blame him for being a boy, you know! He can't help that, and there are some very nice ones about!"

"Are there?" Polly said. "I'm afraid I don't know any."

Violet looked at her. "Don't go thinking we hate men, you know, just 'cos we stand up for women's rights. Well, there's some might do, but I en't one of them. There's men in our movement, too – male suffragists!"

"Oh!" said Polly, confused.

"One of them, Mr. Pethick-Lawrence, even went to prison and went on hunger strike. You see, Poll, you don't have to be a woman to think us women deserve the vote. Any more'n you have to be poor to think people shouldn't have to starve," Violet explained. "Fair-minded people want the best for everyone."

"Doesn't *every*one want the best for everyone?"

"It would be nice if they did. But lots of folk's only interested in themselves."

She was about to go indoors; Polly hesitated, then said, "Violet?"

"Mm?"

"Yesterday – you know, the – the argument."

"Oh, that." Now it was Violet's turn to look embarrassed. "You mustn't take any notice of us. Go at each other hammer and tongs, we do, sometimes."

"It sounded as if – as if you don't really like each other."

Violet grinned. "Sometimes I could wring Edwina's neck! But it's not because I don't like her. She's been so good to me, and I admire her for what she does, even if I don't always agree. It's the risks she takes, the

way she drives herself! But we're in this together – always have been, always will be."

Polly smiled with relief. Really! The peculiar ways grown-ups behaved! At least with Maurice she knew what to expect.

"Sometimes, you know," Violet went on, "the people you care about most, are the ones you get most angry with. Best go now, or I'll make meself late." Violet turned for the side door, but added over her shoulder, "That list of yours – how about 'Ten reasons why Polly *should* have the vote!'"

Yes, of course. Polly sat on the swing again, and began at once with the new heading.

1. *I think I want the best for everyone, not just for myself.*
2. *I can sometimes be sensible.*
3. *I am loyal to my friends.*
4. *I*

Then, defeated, she paused and sucked her pencil. It would be easier to think of bad things about herself, really: I am not very good at arithmetic. I don't always try hard enough at school. I don't think Mama and Papa can trust me not to do things they wouldn't like if they knew about them.

Chapter Eleven

Lily

The weather continued hot and sunny, as if it had no intention of ever changing; Polly counted the days to Lily's visit, helping Aunt Dorothy to plan outings and surprises. To mark the start of the summer holidays, Mr. and Mrs. Dalby took Maurice and Polly on a boat trip along the Thames, all the way from Chelsea to Greenwich. Gazing from the deck, Polly imagined herself voyaging to hidden reaches of the Amazon, or travelling down the Nile to see pyramids and camels. She forgot to wear her hat, and her nose came out in a sprinkling of freckles, which Mama dabbed with lemon juice to make them fade.

It seemed impossible for Mama to get any bigger, but the baby bulge continued to swell. Feeling, she said, like a galleon in full sail, Mama wore loose, light garments, but the heat made her uncomfortable. She fanned herself as she moved slowly about the flat and garden, saying that she could not wait for Folkestone, and the sea breezes. Polly had to remind herself that Mama's normal size and shape would eventually be restored; it seemed so unlikely. The baby was due at the beginning of August, and the doctor visited regularly, proclaiming that all was well, diagnosing rest and plenty of fluids. Polly hoped the baby would come early, while Lily was here; then maybe she and Lily could take it for walks in its perambulator and pretend to be grown-up aunties.

The good thing about Mama resting so much was that Polly could make several escapes to the flat upstairs, each time with a thrill of defiance. "I thought Violet told me you weren't allowed?" said Edwina; but Edwina, of all people, did not let other people tell her how to behave, so she understood. Polly finished off a whole banner by herself, VOTES FOR WOMEN, and pasted posters to boards which could be carried high. It became her secret project, escaping up the stairs every afternoon if she could. As Violet was out at work at these times, only Edwina was there, and Kitty, who sometimes helped. Occasionally other people called in – usually ladies, but once there was a young man called Leonard, who must be one of the male suffragists Violet had told her about. Certainly, he spoke with just as much certainty and determination as Edwina did.

"I'm definitely going to be a proper suffragette as soon as I'm old enough," Polly announced one afternoon.

"I hope," Edwina said, looking at her over the top of the spectacles she wore for sewing, "it won't be *necessary* to be a suffragette by the time you're grown-up. If women haven't got the vote by then, I shall be very disappointed. You must be a traveller, and come home whenever it's time to vote."

"Mama thinks it's a game," Polly said, "me wanting to be an explorer. Like believing in fairies, something I'll grow out of. She thinks I'll be a wife and mother, just like her. But I don't think I'd be very good at it. Wouldn't you like that?" she added; after all, Edwina was the right sort of age, and so was Violet. "I mean, as well as all the other things you do, of course."

"I would only like it," Edwina said, snipping a thread, "if I met exactly the right man. And I haven't, yet. I don't have time to think about it. Now, what about tea with Lily? Shall we say next Thursday?"

Polly coloured up. "I'm not sure. We're going to be very busy, you see, with Aunt Dorothy."

Edwina shot her a shrewd glance. "Oh. Of course, you're not supposed to consort with a lawbreaker. How silly of me."

Polly nodded, her face hot.

"What a shame." Edwina was sewing on a letter F, with quick darts of her needle. "Well, tell me about Lily. What's she like? What does she want to do when she grows up?"

"Lily *does* want to get married and have children," Polly said confidently. "Four, she wants. But apart from that, she'd like to be a nurse. I should think she'd make a good nurse."

"But perhaps she could be a *doctor*!" Edwina said at once. "Why shouldn't she be?"

"Because girls don't –" Polly began, already knowing how Edwina would respond.

"But girls *will*! One day, Polly, when we achieve our aims, women will have exactly the same chances and choices as men do. Isn't that only right and fair? Think of you and Maurice – you're just as clever, aren't you? Just as sensible? Just as capable of learning new things?"

"Yes. Yes, I am." Polly had never met anyone who

spoke as Edwina did – who made her feel that anything was possible, that she could choose whatever she wanted from a whole world of opportunities.

Polly returned, as usual, just in time before Mama stirred from her afternoon rest, and blinked at her vaguely. "Oh, there you are, darling! I do hope you're not getting bored."

"Oh, not at all, Mama," Polly answered, innocent-faced.

For now, there was one opportunity she wanted more than any other – she must find a way of going on next Saturday's march! After all, she had folded the leaflets, sewn the sashes, pasted the posters – she was almost a part of it, now. How feeble it would be to miss the event itself! But Mama and Papa would never let her go, that was for certain.

CB

At last the long-awaited day came – the day of Lily's arrival. Lily was to travel up by train, accompanied by her father, as her mother was reluctant to leave

Tunbridge Wells for the heat and smoke of London. Polly, desperate to go and meet them at Victoria so as not to miss a single second of Lily's visit, was told that her parents couldn't allow her to loiter in the station on her own, and of course Mama couldn't think of going all that way in the heat. The only solution was to persuade Maurice to go with her, "as your escort" was the way Mama put it, though Polly thought of him more as cumbersome baggage. As Maurice liked trains and stations, he agreed quite readily; and they managed to walk all the way to Victoria with only one small argument breaking out, about whether or not Maurice would be able to go on hunger strike and submit to force-feeding, the way Edwina had on her first spell in Holloway.

"I can't see what would be so bad about it," Maurice stated. "All you'd have to do would be lie there. I've had a tooth out, and it can't be nearly as bad as that."

"That's all you know! Violet told me – because

Edwina told *her*, though she's never talked to me about it – it was the most awful agony. Can you imagine? Having tubes forced down your throat and into your stomach, nearly choking you – people holding you down so you can't even struggle, then horrible stuff like gruel pumped in – and the tubes ripped out again afterwards? It was the prison doctor doing it, only you'd never have thought so from how rough he was, Violet said. Edwina only had it once, but some of the suffragettes have had it done to them time and time again. Don't you think they were brave?"

"Brave, or stupid? None of them *had* to have force-feeding – they could have given in and eaten for themselves. They want to make themselves martyrs, that's what my mother says!"

"You have to be brave to be a martyr," Polly said stubbornly.

Maurice was silent for a moment; then, to her surprise, he said, "Yes. All right, then. They *are* brave, to go through all that when they didn't have to."

He had surprised her in another way, too. Two days ago, in the garden, she had boasted to him about her afternoon visits to the flat upstairs. The moment the words were out of her mouth, she had regretted it; but Maurice had not, apparently, said a word to his mother. Polly was forced to think that maybe even Maurice had his good points.

They reached Victoria, and found the right platform. "I do hope they haven't missed their train!" fretted Polly; but there, already, was Lily, waving, and walking as fast as she could towards the barrier, outpacing her father, who was struggling with a number of bags and cases.

"Polly! Polly!"

The two girls hugged; when they broke apart, Lily said, "Oh, hello, Maurice. I didn't know you'd be here."

"Maurice came with me," Polly explained, "otherwise Mama wouldn't have let me come."

Lily was wearing a new dress of kingfisher blue,

with a low waist and a white collar; her well-brushed fair hair was caught back in matching turquoise ribbons. Polly couldn't help thinking that she already looked a little taller and more grown-up than when they had last met; was that possible, in such a short time?

"She's brought enough luggage for a whole family for a fortnight," Lily's father said cheerfully, catching up.

Everything was stowed in a taxicab; then all four of them took their seats and were conveyed in style to Wellington Square.

"Er, I might as well go home, then," Maurice said awkwardly, while Mr. Bradshaw paid the cab driver, and Aunt Dorothy came out to greet the arrivals with cries of delight. Polly had almost forgotten about him.

"Oh, do come and join us for tea!" cried Aunt Dorothy, but Maurice said that he was expected at home, and slipped away.

Shortly afterwards, Lily's father left to catch his

train back, and now Lily and Polly could talk properly – about Lily's new school, and what it was like living in Tunbridge Wells, with the shops and the Pump Room and the Common, and how tedious Polly was finding Maudie Marchant, and the novelty of having suffragettes living upstairs.

"Oh, how exciting!" exclaimed Aunt Dorothy. "I do so admire them!"

"My mother doesn't. Neither does Mrs. Dalby," said Polly. "But I do. They're my friends, you know," she added importantly.

"Now, girls," Aunt Dorothy swept on, "we've got so many lovely things to look forward to! I'm getting tickets for *Swan Lake* – we can all go, you too, Polly –"

"It's going to be such fun!" Lily couldn't keep still. "Polly, come up and see my room. You can help me unpack my things."

At last they were alone together: just like old times, when they'd giggled and chattered in Lily's bedroom or Polly's, trying on their mothers' hats, pretending to be very grand, and striking poses in front of the mirror. Aunt Dorothy's spare bedroom was very pretty and girlish, as if decorated specially for Lily: white candlewick bedspreads; curtains sprigged with rosebuds, and matching cushions; a bedside lamp in clouded glass, shaped like a bluebell flower. "Two beds!" said Lily, flumping down on one and kicking up her feet. "Maybe you could come and stay – wouldn't that be fun?" Quickly she sprang up again: "I must hang up my new dress before it gets creased."

From her suitcase she produced more things Polly hadn't seen before: a party dress in ruby velvet, and bar shoes to go with it, with jet-button fastenings. "For going to concerts and smart occasions like that," she explained.

"You've got a lot of new clothes," Polly remarked. She couldn't help feeling that Lily had overtaken her, and was rushing on into grown-up-ness.

"Well, there are such lovely shops in Tunbridge Wells! Just wait till you come and see them. Your dress is quite nice too, Polly. Now tell me all about these suffragettes! I do hope I'll meet them!"

Before Polly knew what time it was, Papa arrived to collect her on his way home from the bank, and she and Lily had to say goodbye to each other until tomorrow.

"I hope you thanked Maurice for going with you to the station?" Papa said, in Flood Street.

Polly felt herself going hot. She hadn't said a word in thanks. She had hardly even said goodbye to him, so eager had she been to hear all Lily's news – and after he had behaved quite nicely, for once. "I'll go and see him now," she mumbled.

While Papa went in at the side entrance, Polly went round to the front, through the gates, and rang the Dalbys' bell. It was Elsie, the gossip, who answered. Polly gave her a stony look, and asked for Maurice.

Elsie showed her in: across the tiled hall that Mama so envied, and up the stairs that led nowhere. There was a halfway landing here, then three stairs that led straight into a blank wall. Before the house had been converted into flats, this had been the grand stairway leading to all the floors. Now, the landing was an odd in-between place, a dead end, a sort of hidey-hole, and Maurice often left out his games here, or his chess set. He was busy lining up two armies of model soldiers: one side in bright scarlet, the other in royal blue, facing each other across the Turkish red carpet.

"Maurice." Polly paused two stairs short of the landing, and cleared her throat. "I came to say, you know, thank you for coming to the station."

Maurice looked up from his manoeuvres, puzzled, as if he'd already forgotten about it. "Oh, that's all right. Hey, Pegs, what d'you think of the news?"

"What news?"

"There's going to be a *war*!" he announced. "My father says so!"

"In Ireland?"

"No. In Europe. Haven't you seen the newspapers?"

"No."

"Well, you should look at them, then. You know about the shooting of the Archduke of Austria a couple of weeks ago?"

"In that place called – what was it – Sarah-something?" Polly remembered the news-stands.

"You mean Sarajevo, in the Balkans."

"Why does that mean there's got to be a war?"

"You wouldn't understand." Maurice gave her one of his lofty, *you're only a girl* looks that made Polly want to hit him.

"Go on, then! Tell me why, if you know all about it!"

Maurice sat back, folding his arms. "Well, it's complicated. My father says Austria is looking for any chance to declare war on Serbia, and this is it. Then it's about all the countries supporting each other, like teams. Germany's on the same side as Austria. Russia will support Serbia. And we'll be in it, too, because we're on the same side as Russia and Serbia. No one can stay out."

"That doesn't sound very likely to me," Polly scoffed.

"All because of one shooting? So this is the war, is it?" She indicated the red and blue armies at her feet. "They're just – dolls for boys, that's all they are!" With her toe, she pushed over two of the royal blues, so that they fell face-down on the carpet.

"It is! You wait and see." Maurice scrambled to pick up his fallen soldiers, going red in the face – the way he did very easily, Polly had noticed. "And if there *is* a war, and it goes on long enough, I'm going to be in it!"

Chapter Twelve

Plotters

Polly was finding it hard to keep up with Lily's new, consuming interest in clothes and fashions. As Aunt Dorothy shared her niece's passion, they spent a whole afternoon in Selfridges, the huge new store, grand as a museum, which Lily and Aunt Dorothy both thought the next thing to Paradise. "Everything under one roof!" marvelled Aunt Dorothy. "You could spend all day in here!"

They rode the escalators from floor to floor, gazing at the glittering array of goods for sale, from shoes to chandeliers. "It's like Aladdin's cave!" Polly said, content just to wander; she lingered in the toy department, but Lily dismissed that as "for children" and swept on to *Fashions for the Modern Miss*. Eventually, after much trying on and several changes of mind, Lily bought a hat and a silk shantung dress; Aunt Dorothy bought a blouse, and a box of lace-trimmed handkerchieves for Lily's mother. For the sake of joining in, Polly decided to spend her pocket money on new hair ribbons. Dazzled by a rainbow of tempting colours displayed glossily in a drawer, she was about to choose pale lilac, but changed her mind at the last moment and picked green, white and purple.

"You'd have done better with the lavender," Lily remarked. "That was a perfect match for the stripes in your blouse."

"These are suffragette colours! Green for hope, white for purity, purple for dignity."

"I know that! But I don't see why you've wasted your money – you can hardly wear them to school. And your mother won't let you wear them when she's around."

Polly didn't care. The point was to *have* the ribbons – a private expression of her loyalty to Violet and Edwina.

Tired from all the shopping, they had cakes and lemonade in the restaurant, and afterwards walked towards Marble Arch, for the bus home.

"Couldn't we go over there, just for a little while?" asked Polly, attracted by the greenness of Hyde Park.

"My feet ache," Lily complained, but Aunt Dorothy thought it was a good idea.

"We can walk down to the Serpentine, and catch a bus from Knightsbridge."

They crossed Park Lane, dodging motorcars and omnibuses, horses and bicycles, and entered the park at what Aunt Dorothy said was Speaker's Corner. Polly looked around her, seeing nothing but a bare space with railings on three sides, and trodden dust.

"Oh! This is where –"

"Yes, that's right," said Aunt Dorothy. "Where anyone can stand up on a soapbox and make a speech."

"Could we do it now?" Polly asked, imagining herself, at this very moment, launching into an address about votes for women. How would people react? There weren't all that many people around to listen – a few strollers, a nursemaid with twins in a perambulator, a family having a picnic. How foolish she would feel!

"Well, you could," said Aunt Dorothy, laughing. "But I think there are special times. If you're going to start airing your views, you need an audience. I've heard Mrs. Pankhurst speak here, you know. Very stirring, she was – but there were those in the crowd who booed and jeered at her. A lot of courage, it must take, to stand up and expose yourself to ridicule. I'm quite sure I couldn't do it!"

"You're not a suffragette, are you, Aunt Dorothy?" asked Lily, swinging her shopping bags.

Aunt Dorothy shook her head. "No," she said, with a small sigh. "I half wish I were – I take my hat off to them. But, well, I've got my living to make. Who'd send me their daughters for piano lessons, if I were out on the streets smashing windows and setting buildings on fire?"

"Miss Rutherford's going to make a speech here," Polly said. "Edwina, who I told you about, who lives in Lily's old flat. And there's going to be a march to Chelsea Town Hall – a parade. It's on Saturday." The idea seized her. "You wouldn't want to miss it, would you?" she appealed to Aunt Dorothy.

"A parade?" said Lily. "We might as well come and see it. Can't we, Auntie?"

"Well, I don't know. Not with my reputation to think of."

"Oh, you don't need to worry about that," Polly assured her. "No one's going to smash windows or set fire to things, not on a *parade*. We could just walk along with them, just for a little way. If we went back to Selfridges and you bought coloured ribbons, like mine," she added to Lily, "we could both put them round our straw hats."

"So we'd match, and we could do our hair the same, as well! Yes, do let's!" Lily turned to her aunt. "It would be an awful shame to miss it, when it's so close. We can come, can't we, the three of us?"

Aunt Dorothy still looked doubtful. "Whatever would your parents say?"

"Invite Polly to stay the night," Lily urged her; "then we needn't tell her parents, or mine."

Aunt Dorothy was hesitating, Polly could see. "It would be wrong of me to let you keep secrets from your parents."

Polly had an idea. "I know! We could just happen to be here in the park on Saturday, having a picnic, say, and we'll wander over to see what's going on, and – no one could blame us for that, could they?"

"Go on, Auntie – say yes." Lily put on her most appealing expression, head on one side. "If they *ask*, then we'll tell them – but they won't. No one will mind us having a picnic in the park, and looking at a parade that just happens to be starting off."

"And we won't have to tell even the smallest lie!" added Polly.

"Oh dear, you two!" Aunt Dorothy laughed. "Determined to get me into trouble, the pair of you!"

Polly took a few skipping steps. "Does that mean we can go?"

"Well! I would like to show a bit of support. We'll see."

Did *all* grown-ups say that, Polly wondered? But there was a difference: when Mama said it, it sounded like No; the way Aunt Dorothy just had, it sounded a lot more like Yes.

☙

It was one of the best weeks Polly could remember. Aunt Dorothy, glad of the girls' company, was quite happy for Polly to spend nearly all the time at Wellington Square. Polly's mother, with the Folkestone holiday to plan as well as all the knitting and sewing she was doing for the baby, did not mind her spending so much time with Lily. A visit to Regent's Park Zoo; a tour of the city on an open-topped bus; a tea party with some cousins of Lily's, and *Swan Lake*, which was so beautiful that it brought tears to Polly's eyes, and made Lily decide that she wanted to be a prima ballerina: "I'm going to ask Mama if I can take ballet lessons," she announced. Even Polly daydreamed about pirouetting on a stage and astonishing everyone with her grace, beauty and skill, even though she knew full well that she was far too clumsy.

The week rushed past. At the end of it, like a birthday cake waiting for its candles to be lit, was the march. Busy with Lily and the rush of activity, Polly wasn't able to help with any more preparations, but she did sneak upstairs one morning to push a note under Edwina's and Violet's door: *Good luck for*

Saturday! I will be there at Speaker's Corner and all the way to the Town Hall! Could I have three sashes, please? You could hide them under the blackcurrant bushes.

The very next morning, there were the three bright sashes, tied into a neat package, with a note from Violet: Well done! I will see you there.

"I've hardly seen you this week," grumbled Maurice, when Mama sent Polly downstairs with a message for Mrs. Dalby. He was playing chess, by himself, on the landing-space, which struck Polly as a rather pointless thing to do.

"Good job, too!" she retorted. "I expect you've missed having someone to tease."

"Mother says, would you and Lily and her aunt like to come to tea on Sunday?"

"Maybe, if there's time." Polly couldn't think as far as Sunday. Saturday came first, jostling to the front of her mind, blocking out all other days beyond. Saturday was a suffragette day, not a red-letter day but a green, white and purple day; the first day of her new career as campaigner for women's rights.

She took the sashes to Wellington Square. Showing them to Lily and Aunt Dorothy made her feel like a proper suffragette.

"I can hardly wait!" Lily kept saying. "It's going to be so *exciting*!"

"Yes, but –" Polly wasn't sure Lily was taking the campaign seriously enough. "It's not just about having fun. It's about standing up for what's right. It's about wanting things to be fair – not wanting to be second-best!"

"I know *that*," Lily said, fingering the sash. "Do you think my white lace blouse would look nice with this? Or the cream one with the sailor collar?"

Aunt Dorothy smiled, and caught Polly's eye. "I don't think you're quite cut out for political campaigning, Lily, somehow!"

"Oh, but I am," Lily protested. "Christabel Pankhurst's *very* fashionable, Mama says. I don't see why one should look a fright when one's marching about the streets – who would take any notice?"

At last Saturday came. Early, Polly packed a small bag with her overnight things.

"I'm wondering if you really need stay overnight with Mrs. Langrish, after all," said Mama, coming into her bedroom. "It's very kind of her, but it puts her to a lot of extra trouble."

"Oh, no," said Polly quickly. "She really doesn't mind at all, and the spare bed's already made up."

"Your father's dining out on Saturday evening, too," Mama said, a little wistfully. "I shall be here all on my own."

"Oh, but I've been so looking forward to it, Mama – and it's Lily's last night, before she goes home!"

Mama sighed. "You're going to miss her," she said gently. "No doubt the two of you want to stay awake talking half the night. Well, I suppose it won't hurt, for once."

Polly felt guilty for deceiving her; but suffragettes

had to make plans, didn't they, secret plans? And, after all, she was only going to walk along a street, not set fire to Mr. Asquith's new golfing villa, or slash a famous painting in the Royal Academy, or throw flour at the Lord Mayor. She knew from Edwina that there were all sorts of plots, more and more of them, ever-ingenious: all to keep the Cause "in the public eye", as Edwina put it.

By the time she left, with Papa carrying her bag, she felt herself almost fizzing with concealed excitement. She was going on the march now, and nothing could stop her.

Chapter Thirteen

Purple, White and Green

"I'm not sure this is such a good idea," Aunt Dorothy said doubtfully.

They were crossing the road towards Speaker's Corner. Already there was quite a gathering, and people were drifting across the park to see what was going on.

"It'll be all right, Auntie," said Lily.

"Well, I hope so. Now, you must stay with me,

both of you, not go running off and getting into trouble."

"As if we would!" Lily gave her an impatient look. "Have you got the sashes, Polly?"

"In the picnic basket."

They stopped by the railings, and Aunt Dorothy took out the three sashes. In her bag she also had the rather simple picnic – cucumber sandwiches, apples and a bottle of lemonade – which was their excuse for being in Hyde Park. Polly felt a swell of pride as she pulled the sash over her head and one arm, and adjusted it against her blouse. Lily, who had finally decided on the white lace, put hers on too, and tilted her hat, with its ribbon band, first one way and then the other.

"Come on! There's no time for primping! I want to see Edwina and Violet." Polly tugged at Lily's arm, moving in the direction of the wooden platform for the speakers; she scanned the faces beneath straw hats decked with suffragette colours. The crowd was mainly women, with only a few men. Among them Polly recognized Leonard, the young man who had visited Edwina; he was holding a megaphone by his side, and talking earnestly to a tall woman who wore a badge marked *Steward*. Posters on boards, like the ones Polly had helped to make, were stacked against the railings, ready to be held aloft.

Aunt Dorothy had met someone she knew, and was standing talking on the edge of the crowd; Lily was waiting for her, looking towards the platform. Polly moved on, keeping an eye on them. Being in the middle of all this, in the warm sunshine, surrounded by people waving and calling out and greeting each other, felt like being at a party – a very special kind of party. She stood for a moment in a rush of happiness, taking it all in: the sun bright on straw hats and white dresses, the flashes of purple, green and white that linked everyone, the dappled sunshine under the plane trees, the scream of swifts high in the blue, cloud-wisped sky, the clop of hooves on Park Lane, an engine sputtering and the honk of a car horn, someone shouting from a van, the voices around her, the sense of anticipation; she felt she were living as she had never lived before. If I'm going to be a suffragette, she thought, then this is where I'll belong – with women, with people like these, who are prepared to march the streets to stand up for what they believe in.

More and more people were pressing into the area; Lily caught up, grabbing Polly's arm. Polly had to crane her neck to see past the adults surrounding her. Lily, taller, was able to see better, and turned to wave to her aunt: "We're here!" She waved energetically, and Aunt Dorothy pushed her way towards them. "Someone's getting up on the box," Lily reported, "she's going to speak – she's got the megaphone –"

Shushings silenced the crowd, and Polly, craning, saw a tall woman – not Edwina, someone older and more weathered – facing her audience. "Ladies – and gentlemen! May I have your attention, please?" More shushings, fingers held to lips, till all conversations were silenced and everyone faced the speaker. "We of the WSPU," the woman went on, in a loud, confident voice, "are delighted to see such a turnout today – here in Hyde Park, the scene of many glorious rallies in the last few years. In a few minutes we will move off across the park, and on to Sloane Square and the King's Road. Please keep together. I must stress that we want no incident of any kind until we reach Chelsea Town Hall, so please do not respond to any provocation from bystanders. There will be police in attendance, of course, but also our own stewards, who will walk beside and behind the procession. In a moment we will be addressed by one of our comrades who has done so much to organize this march and countless other protests; at the Town Hall there will be more speeches until we are compelled to disperse, while six of our number attempt to enter the building and demand an audience with the Mayor. Thank you again for your support. Now, it is a great honour for me to introduce a most respected member of our sisterhood – Miss Edwina Rutherford."

Applause and cheers broke out as Edwina mounted the box. She seemed to stumble as she stepped up; regained her balance and took the megaphone from the first speaker.

Lily nudged Polly. "Is that her?"

Polly felt so proud that a lump in her throat made it hard to swallow. She nodded, balancing on tiptoe; she fixed her eyes on Edwina, who straightened and paused, surveying the crowd for a few moments without speaking. Then she began: "Thank you, Miss Selby. I would like to add my own thanks to hers for this magnificent turnout." Her voice was quiet and calm; the effect on the audience was that everyone stood hardly moving, focusing their full attention on the slight figure with the megaphone. "Gatherings like these," Edwina continued, "can leave the government in no doubt about the strength of our determination. Petitions with over a million signatures have now been handed in at the House of Commons. Take heed, Prime Minister Asquith" – she turned, as if sending her words over the heads of her audience in the direction of Westminster – "if you will not listen to us, we will *make* you listen! We will not be ignored; we will never give up the fight. For how can we give up our struggle, go back to being dutiful mothers, daughters, wives and workers, when the government insists on treating us as second-class citizens? When we are—"

"Stand back. Stand back," a loud male voice cut in; there was a surge in the crowd behind Polly, and she turned to see four helmeted policemen pushing towards the front. "Make way. Madam, please stand aside. I must insist you give way."

Edwina must have seen the disturbance, but she carried on, barely faltering: "– when we are denied the rights given to any man who happens to –"

Polly found herself pushed aside, off balance, by the swell of movement, as people tried to push in different directions – some merely trying to get out of the way, others defiantly blocking the path of the policemen. One woman began battering the arm of the largest policeman with her fists; he grabbed her bodily and pushed her out of his way, where she overbalanced and fell, hauled to her feet by other women nearby.

"Oh, what's –" Lily clutched Polly's arm for support.

The crowd around them, orderly and still a few moments before, was now turbulent with cross-currents. Polly felt panic rising. Never in her life had she been in the middle of such a crowd; never before had she feared being accidentally crushed or trampled. "They've come for Edwina!" she gasped to Lily. "She knew they would – she'll be taken back to prison –"

"Then why did she come? She didn't have to –"

Hemmed in on all sides, Polly tried to see what was happening. Only four policemen, in this crowd – so outnumbered, how could they succeed? But, glancing behind her, Polly saw another line of police by the Park Lane railings – reinforcements, intimidating, with their uniforms, helmets and truncheons. Only a few of the women were brave enough to attack the officers with fists or placards or, in one or two cases, with clubs they must have hidden under their skirts. More policemen shoved through to catch hold of these women and take them to the rear. Polly glimpsed one of them, kicking and shouting as a large policeman lifted her bodily off the ground.

"Girls, girls, come away, let's move back under the trees –" Aunt Dorothy was trying to reach them, grabbing Lily's sleeve. Lily moved towards her aunt, looking round for Polly, but Polly, anxious to see what had happened to Edwina, pretended not to notice.

"Excuse me – I've got to –" Gradually, ducking under elbows and between bodies, she made her way nearer to the speaker's platform. Abruptly the breath was slammed out of her lungs as someone lurched back and collided with her. Knocked sideways, she turned awkwardly and felt a wrench of pain in her right ankle. She was down, sprawled on the ground, clutching at someone's skirt as she fell; she glimpsed lace petticoats and dainty shoes, serge trousers and a policeman's heavy boots, then arms reached down and hoisted her upright. "Oops-a-daisy! Are you all right, my duck?" A kindly woman was brushing her down.

Polly nodded, her eyes filling with tears as the sickness of pain reeled through her. She put her right foot to the ground, found that it would still bear her weight – not broken, then, thank goodness! "Thank you," she managed, with a grimacing attempt at a smile, and limped forward.

Edwina carried on speaking into the megaphone until the very last moment. Polly saw her sway and stumble as she was pulled off the box, then handcuffs flashed as she was captured. Edwina did not struggle, did not even try to resist. She held her head high, surrounded by a flock of her closest followers as two policemen led her away towards a black van that waited on Park Lane.

It's what she wanted, Polly realized. She wanted to be handcuffed and led away in full view of everyone. She knew this would happen. If she hadn't wanted it, she could have kept herself hidden.

Some of the women pursued the police van as it drove away, hammering on the roof with their fists, shouting at the policemen inside or with words of encouragement to Edwina. Others, rallied by Miss Selby, who now had the megaphone, were pressing back into Speaker's Corner.

What now? Miss Selby had righted the box and was standing on it, trying to restore order. "We have just seen an example of the Cat and Mouse Act in action," she yelled, "the Liberal government's way of dealing with political protestors! We must not allow this violent interruption to hinder our peaceful proceedings. The march will continue as planned."

Gradually the hubbub faded, as she regained control of the throng. "Miss Rutherford, our brave comrade, was well aware that police would be waiting for her here. She helped plan the protest with this outcome in mind. She will endure another stay in prison with fortitude. Others are here to lead us to Chelsea Town Hall and to confront the Mayor and his party there. Proceed!" she finished dramatically, as if ordering a cavalry into battle.

Polly tested her ankle, hobbling a few steps. Though weakened and painful, it would bear her weight. Everyone was gradually moving and shuffling, marshalled by stewards, into a massed column on Broad Walk. Polly could no longer see Aunt Dorothy or Lily; she thought they had moved back towards the railings. Deliberately she did not look round: if Aunt Dorothy saw that she was injured, there would be no question of marching even a short way. Having got this far, Polly was determined not to give up, even if the distance from here to Chelsea Town Hall now seemed a very long way indeed. She slipped into the column, surrounding herself with taller people.

Posters were held aloft, banners raised, purple, white and green, giving a festive air as the procession moved off. "Votes for women!" someone shouted at the front, and the cry was taken up by others. Progress was a slow shamble at first, almost treading on the heels of people in front, then accelerating to the brisk pace set by the stewards. At first, Polly's injured foot made her wince with each step, but the pain soon began to lessen.

"Get back to your kitchen sinks!" a passer-by yelled from Park Lane.

"Should be locked up, the lot of you!" someone else shouted. And one of the marching women called back, "We will be, if that's what it costs!"

Polly felt herself bubbling inside with pride and excitement, willing to march for miles and miles. She would hop on one foot, if necessary! The taunters were on the other side of the railings; she was on this side, surrounded by strong-minded women. She would do it. Nothing would stop her now. She was marching with the suffragettes, and she felt that nothing in her life so far had been as worthwhile.

Chapter Fourteen

Caught

By the time the procession had passed through the park, and was moving down Sloane Street, it had attracted attention of various kinds. A group of boys ran up and down the length of the column, screaming taunts; someone threw a tomato, which burst squashily against one of the poster boards and left a juicy trail of pips on the hats of the two nearest women; some bystanders laughed, or just turned to stare. But others applauded, or shouted, "Good luck to you!"

Polly had not seen Lily or Aunt Dorothy since the marchers had moved off. By now, she was trying to squash a feeling of guilty unease beneath her excitement. The urge to join the marchers had been so irresistible that she'd almost forgotten what she'd told Aunt Dorothy about just looking, or about walking only a little way. Where were they? Somewhere behind, she assumed – but they would be worried, having lost her in the scuffle at Speaker's Corner. How was she going to find them again? A woman walking beside her asked kindly, "Excuse me, my dear, but I can't help feeling anxious – are you all on your own? Is your mother not with you?"

"No," Polly replied; "I'm with my friend and her aunt. They're coming along behind."

"And you seem to be limping – have you blistered your foot, dear, with all this walking?"

Polly shook her head and shrugged off the

sympathy, but felt a little less alone. This woman was quite old, older than Polly's grandmother, with white hair and a lined face, but was striding out as purposefully as anyone.

In the King's Road, people came out of shops and stood in doorways to watch. The procession took up the width of the street, bringing traffic to a standstill. Whether Polly looked ahead or behind, all she could see was a mass of heads, beribboned hats, the banners proclaiming VOTES FOR WOMEN, and the placards bobbing like marker buoys in a harbour. At the Town Hall – the grand new building with its classical pillared entrances and its gilded clock – everything became a little confused. Everyone wanted to get as close to the steps as possible, but the helmeted heads of policemen could be seen above the crush of people, intent on keeping the roadway clear so that the Mayor and his guests could enter the building. Afraid of being knocked over again, Polly found a safe place to stand, on the corner of Chelsea

Manor Street, which gave her a good view of the proceedings. It had been hot and tiring, walking in the heat; she felt sweat trickling inside her blouse, her feet unbearably hot, and now that she had stopped walking, her ankle was throbbing painfully enough to make her feel sick. Maybe she had injured it more badly than she thought after all, and all the walking was making it worse.

For the first time she saw Violet, with a group standing on the far side of the entrance. One of them held a large sealed letter, for the Mayor, Polly presumed. Of Lily and Aunt Dorothy there was no sign, but if they had been towards the back of the procession it would be difficult for them to get anywhere near the Town Hall steps.

Numbers of police now formed a semi-circular barricade to keep the entrance clear. Guests were starting to arrive, walking from taxicabs drawn up as close as they could get – gentlemen in tail coats and bow ties, and jewelled ladies in evening dresses, some wrapped in shawls in spite of the evening's warmth. They picked their way carefully, guided by police; some gave disdainful looks at the mass of women. Polly saw that the kind white-haired woman who had spoken to her on the march had positioned herself close enough to the police cordon to reach out an arm and offer a leaflet to each person who approached the entrance. Most simply ignored her; one man accepted a leaflet and gave it a disparaging glance before crumpling it in his hand and tossing it to the ground. Only one of the guests, a gracious-looking woman in dark red with a tasselled silk wrap, took a leaflet and smiled her thanks before being guided up the steps by a policeman.

Polly knew that everyone was waiting for the Mayor himself – or was he already inside? She was hoping for a magnificently grand entrance. Maybe he would arrive in a carriage drawn by six black horses, and would be resplendent in scarlet, bedecked with chains of office. But now everything was happening at once. She saw Violet, with two other women, duck beneath the arms of the unsuspecting policemen to rush for the steps, Violet in the lead, holding the sealed letter. A stir of excitement rippled through the waiting crowd. The liveried footman at the door gave a yell, and a constable leaped up to tackle Violet from behind.

"Listen to our demands!" someone yelled, and more voices joined in with, "Votes for women!"

Another voice shrilled through the chanting. "Polly! Polly!" It was Aunt Dorothy, trying to move towards her from the other side of the police cordon; Polly glimpsed Lily's anxious face beside her, straining to see. Now more guests were arriving, two gentlemen and a woman; Violet and her two companions had been bundled to one side of the entrance. Polly stood undecided, while Aunt Dorothy called again, more urgently.

The new guests passed so close that she registered a waft of flowery perfume. The taller of the two men, dressed in dinner jacket and black tie like the others, stopped in astonishment before reaching the steps.

"*Polly!* What, in God's name –"

Polly's heart pounded; she swayed, and put a hand against the wall to steady herself. Of all people, she had not expected to see Papa.

Chapter Fifteen

Disgrace

When Papa was displeased, he seemed to Polly like a cold stranger. This time he was more than displeased; he was almost white with anger. And the person he was most angry with was Aunt Dorothy.

He had excused himself from the Mayor's reception and led Polly down the King's Road, hailing the first taxicab he saw. Aunt Dorothy hurried after them to explain, but all Papa said, tight-lipped and aloof, was: "My wife and I entrusted you with the care of our daughter, and you brought her to this – this scrimmage. That's as much as I need to know. We will discuss this tomorrow."

What made it even worse was that Polly's ankle had now stiffened badly, after all the walking and then standing still, and she could barely hobble, supported by her father's arm. At home, there was more shock and dismay from Mama, a barrage of questions, and Polly was made to sit on the sofa with her ankle propped on a cushioned footstool, while Dr. Mayes was summoned, and Mrs. Parks fetched cold flannels. Her injury at least protected her from the worst of Papa's wrath, but she could not hold back the hot tears that spilled down her cheeks. The dizzy excitement of earlier this evening had turned to this – pain, anger, difficult explanations.

"So," Papa persisted, "That Woman" (for this was what Aunt Dorothy had now become) "deliberately deceived us, led us to believe you were spending a quiet evening at her home with Lily, then led you into that street brawl?"

"No! It wasn't her fault!" Polly said hotly. "It was all my idea – I wanted to go, and I persuaded her to take us – and I promised to stay with her and not get into trouble –"

"Mrs. Langrish must take the blame, though, Polly," said Mama. "She was in charge of you, and Lily. I don't imagine Lily's parents will be at all pleased when they hear about it, either. It really was very irresponsible of Mrs. Langrish, when she must have known that neither we nor Lily's parents would have allowed it."

"It's utterly disgraceful!" Papa almost spat the words. "Your mother must find you another piano teacher, Polly – and I shall call tomorrow to tell That Woman exactly what I think of her conduct. I'm surprised she isn't more careful of her reputation."

"As for letting you tramp miles through the streets with a sprained ankle –" Mama bent to examine it again, shaking her head.

"She didn't! I didn't even tell her, and I set off ahead of her and Lily so that she wouldn't find out."

Papa's expression became even sterner. "So you were *unaccompanied* on the march? Polly, this is sounding worse and worse."

They were interrupted by the arrival of Dr. Mayes, who examined Polly's ankle, turning it this way and that, and asked her to wriggle her toes.

"Nothing broken," he pronounced. "But you've wrenched it badly. There will be bruising and swelling, nothing worse. Rest for you, young lady, until the swelling starts to subside, and cold compresses will help. I'd give her some hot, sweet tea now, for the shock," he added to Mama.

In bed at last, uncomfortably turning her ankle this way and that to avoid the pressure from the bedclothes, Polly realized that she had scarcely given a thought to Violet or Edwina. Edwina had been driven away in the van, presumably back to Holloway; but what of Violet, last seen in the grip of a policeman at the entrance to the Town Hall? Polly listened intently for any creak of floorboards from the flat above, but heard nothing. How was she to find out? It would be no use asking Mama or Papa, and there was no chance of going upstairs. What if Violet had been arrested, too? And as for Lily – Polly had no idea how she was going to see Lily again, before she left for Tunbridge Wells. Her parents had made it clear that she wasn't going anywhere, not even downstairs for tea with Maurice. It would be awful for Lily's stay to end like this, without even the chance to say goodbye to each other.

In the morning her foot had stiffened so badly that she could only hop. She was excused going to church, but her parents went as usual, leaving her in Mrs. Parks' charge. "You're not to move from this sofa," Mama instructed, handing her a prayer book. "And since you can't come with us, I suggest you spend the time reading this instead."

Polly was unable to concentrate on reading the Prayer Book or anything else. Smells of roasting meat drifted in from the kitchen, and she could hear Mrs. Parks humming as she worked, clattering pans, setting the table in the dining room. After gazing at a single page for some minutes without taking in a word of it, an idea occurred to her.

Still humming cheerfully in a way she would never do if Polly's parents were at home, Mrs. Parks entered the room with a glass of milk and a sugared biscuit for Polly.

"Mrs. Parks," Polly asked, "do you ever talk to Kitty – you know, the maid upstairs?"

"Indeed I do," replied Mrs. Parks, plumping up the sofa cushions. "She's my niece."

"Your *niece*!"

It had never occurred to Polly to think about Mrs. Parks' family life. She was an indispensable part of the household, the person who made sure there was food in the larder, meals on the table, and freshly laundered clothes to wear, and that was as far as Polly usually considered. Now that she thought about it, she had a vague idea that Mrs. Parks had a son, and presumably a husband.

"It was through me Kitty got that job," Mrs. Parks continued. "I knew the young ladies was looking for a maid-housekeeper, and I thought it would suit Kitty, so I spoke to them about her. She's very happy with them. Now, I must start cooking the vegetables, or there won't be any dinner."

All these lives going on, Polly thought, so close to her own, yet she knew so little about them! "Mrs. Parks," she said, "can you do something for me? Can you find out from Kitty what happened to Violet and Edwina yesterday? I don't know if Violet's come home – whether she's –"

Mrs. Parks glanced out of the open window. "Here's your ma and pa now, with the Dalbys – I must get on. Yes, all right, Miss Polly," she added in a low voice. "I'll do my best."

Polly picked up the prayer book, arranged herself demurely on the sofa and pretended to be absorbed in reading. It would take a few moments for Mama and Papa to go round to the side entrance and up the stairs. While she composed herself, she heard loud voices in the front garden: several of them, voices raised in dispute, and one that sounded like Lily's. She swung herself off the sofa and limped painfully to the window.

Her parents, with Mr. and Mrs. Dalby and Maurice, were inside the wrought-iron gates; they must be going in with the Dalbys, as they occasionally did, for a glass of sherry. Outside, trying to come through, were Aunt Dorothy and Lily. Papa had pushed the gates closed.

"I will not allow it!" Tall, haughty, he barred the way. "Please leave the premises. Polly is not well enough for visitors, and I don't want her to see Lily again during her stay. That is to be her punishment."

"O-oh!" Lily wailed. "Please let me come in, only for a few minutes! I'm going home today, and it's my last chance!"

"I have said no, Lily, and no is what I mean. I have no intention of arguing about it in the public street."

"We only wanted to see how she is, and bring her bag back!" Aunt Dorothy tried.

Papa reached for the bag. "Thank you," he said coldly; then closed and latched the gates. "Mrs. Langrish, I give you notice that we will be finding another piano teacher for Polly. I have forbidden her to return to Wellington Square. Good day."

Mama hadn't said a word. She followed Papa as he turned towards the door, following the Dalbys. Aunt Dorothy and Lily stood for a few moments, looking at them over the fence; then, as Polly watched, they turned away.

Polly opened the window wider. "Lily!" she shouted.

Lily stopped and looked round; Polly saw that she was crying.

"*Polly!*" Papa turned to face the first-floor window, his face rigid with anger. "Close that window at once!"

"I'll write to you!" Polly yelled to Lily.

"Did you hear me, young madam!" Papa wasn't shouting; he spoke in what was almost a stage whisper, but Polly heard him clearly enough.

"Best do what your pa says, lovey," said Mrs. Parks' quiet voice behind her. "You don't want to go asking for even more trouble."

Chapter Sixteen

Seaside Holiday

Polly was bored with staying indoors. She had been forbidden to go out, partly because of her swollen ankle, partly as punishment; and of course Papa was even crosser with her, now that she had defied him by shouting from the window. She played the piano, badly and half-heartedly; she wrote a letter to Aunt Dorothy to say she was sorry, and one to Lily, and asked Maurice to post them for her in secret. No one came to see her, apart from Maurice; no Lily, no Aunt Dorothy, and no chance at all of speaking to Violet. Lily had gone back to Tunbridge Wells, leaving Polly with no idea when she was ever going to see her again. Everything had gone dull and flat since the march. And, as Mrs. Parks reminded her, the suffragettes had been campaigning for years for the vote; why should they succeed now?

Wasn't it exciting, though? Lily wrote from Tunbridge Wells. *Even if we did get into trouble. Even if you did go marching off on your own and didn't even wait for me, which was rather bad of you, frankly. But I will be generous and believe that you were overwhelmed by the occasion. Your papa was really quite beastly about it, but my mother says she will write to him herself and tell him that it was partly my fault for persuading Aunt Dorothy, and she thinks that if she asks really nicely he will relent and let you come and stay with us for two weeks later on. He and your mother will*

*be completely taken up with the new baby, Mama
says, so they will be glad to have you off their hands.*

The thought of the new baby taking up everyone's
attention did little to improve Polly's mood. Bored,
hot and sulky, she looked out of the dining-room
window. Even the garden looked past its best: wilting
in the heat, the roses dropping faded petals, the grass
browning. Preparations were now being made for
Folkestone – clothes sorted, trunks packed – but Polly
could not even look forward to that, very much. Her
parents' disapproval had now reached a third stage.
Their first reaction had been concern for her injury,
their anger directed at Aunt Dorothy; after Dr. Mayes'
visit, Polly herself had received the full blast of her
father's disapproval, in the form of several lectures on
disobedience and its consequences. Now, that phase
was over, and it seemed to be agreed that Polly's
misdemeanour would never be mentioned again, but
there was a chilly politeness in the air that was almost
worse than being punished.

The only good thing was that Mrs. Parks had kept her promise by finding out what had happened to Violet. In response to Kitty's enquiries, Violet sent a note, which Polly kept hidden in her handkerchief drawer. She had written:

Dear Polly,

I am so sorry to hear you have hurt your ankle. Consider it an honourable injury. We were very pleased with the numbers attending our march, and very grateful to you for coming, even though it turned out badly for you. Although we did not gain admittance to the Town Hall, I did give my letter and petition to an official who promised me he would deliver it personally to the Lord Mayor. Edwina, as you probably saw, was re-arrested and taken back to Holloway, where I shall visit her as soon as it is allowed. I am sure she will resume her hunger strike and will be released when the prison authorities *think she is too weak to continue.*

We are so grateful for your support, Polly, as I know it is difficult for you. If I can see a chance of speaking to you in the garden, I will come down; if not I can send you notes through Kitty to let you know when Edwina is home. I hope your ankle heals quickly and that you have an enjoyable stay at Folkestone. Do let me know when you return.

With sincerest good wishes,
Your friend,
Violet Cross

Polly showed the letter to Maurice, who had become, oddly, a sort of ally. He was rather impressed by the way Polly had contrived to go on the march, and by Edwina's arrest.

"Did they really put handcuffs on her, and haul her off to the van?"

"Yes – and Violet could easily have got herself

arrested, too," Polly told him. "Not for doing anything bad, like attacking someone – just for trying to give a petition to the Lord Mayor!"

"My mother's written another letter to the Earl of Belmont, to say those two shouldn't be allowed to live here. He answered her first one, but didn't say he was going to do anything about it."

Polly looked at him. "Did you hope he would? Did you think he'd turn up here and throw them out onto the street?"

"'Course not. Well," Maurice conceded, "I might have hoped for that at first, but now I think it's interesting, having them here. I'd be sorry if they left. What if Edwina dies? How many times can you starve yourself?"

"I don't know." Polly was unsure whether hunger striking would get easier each time, or harder.

Meanwhile, her parents were behaving as if Edwina and Violet simply didn't exist; as if it would be shameful even to mention them. Maurice and Polly agreed that it was quite ridiculous, the way grown-ups behaved sometimes. Polly trusted Maurice, by now, not to tell his mother about Violet's letter. It was fun, sharing secrets. With Lily gone, Maurice would have to do.

"You might send me a postcard from the seaside," Maurice said, "and bring me back a stick of rock."

"Yes, all right."

"Make sure you get back before the war starts," Maurice warned.

"You and your war!" Polly teased. "You'll be disappointed if it all comes to nothing! Go and play with your soldiers."

"It won't," Maurice said. "You only have to look at the newspapers."

In Folkestone there would not even be Maurice, and although there would be sea and sand, Polly did not see how she was going to enjoy them much, on her own, unable to walk far, and with Mama resting each afternoon. If only Lily could come!

London was so hot and dusty that Polly began to think longingly of rain and fog, of winter nights and drawn curtains, of frost patterns on the windowpanes. It was a relief, at last, to be on the train to Folkestone, looking out at meadows and hills, woods and cornfields and orchards, oast houses with their pointy white hats that Papa said were called cowls, and the sweep of the North Downs. Mama sat fanning herself, half dozing; occasionally her head would nod with sleep till she blinked awake again to gaze uncomprehendingly out of the window. Polly had started a new book, *Little Women*, given to her by Mama. She had finished *Under Desert Skies*, and would have preferred to choose something else from Edwina's crammed bookshelves, but as that was impossible she was reading Mama's choice. She had expected it to be all about girls behaving nicely, and indeed Meg and Beth always did, but she found an unexpected fictional ally in spirited Jo. With her ambition to be an author, Jo was a character Edwina would approve of.

Papa was engrossed in *The Times*. The front page was full of news about armies mobilizing, and ultimatums.

"Papa," Polly asked, "what's an ultimatum, please?"

He lowered the newspaper. "It's a final demand. It means giving someone a last chance to do something, or face reprisals."

"What are reprisals?"

"Reprisals are – well, a sort of punishment. The consequences of doing something, or of not doing something." He gave her a significant look.

"Is there going to be a war?" Polly asked, not wanting the conversation to take a personal turn.

"Oh, it's not settled yet," said Papa, in his *wait-and-see* voice.

At Folkestone they settled themselves into a boarding house on the seafront. The other family staying there had two children much younger than Polly, to her disappointment, and their own nursemaid to look after them. There were strolls along the promenade, a band concert, and on one afternoon a troupe of jugglers and acrobats in the park. Best of all, there was the sea. Polly never tired of it: the ever-changing light, the saltiness on her lips and in her hair, the mesmerizing sound of the waves, the crunch of stones as the undertow sucked back. The gulls screamed with a sound that was at once restless and soothing. She could see ships far out in the Channel, and sometimes, hazily, the coast of France. How odd that it was so near: nearer, Papa said, than home was.

There were soldiers, too, in Folkestone, marching to or from nearby barracks in their khaki uniforms, accompanied by officers on horseback. Polly thought of Maurice. GERMANY DECLARES WAR ON FRANCE was all over the newspaper billboards, in big letters. Papa went out early each morning to buy his copy of *The Times*, and would not go to the promenade or beach till he had read it.

"If there's war between Germany and France, will we be in it?" Polly asked him.

"Well, you see, we're part of a treaty that says Belgium is neutral. If Germany invades Belgium we'll be drawn into the conflict."

It was like a new language, all this talk of alliances and mobilizations, of pacts and treaties. But the day after the Bank Holiday Monday, all the wondering was answered by one simple word: WAR.

Chapter Seventeen

Ends and Beginnings

The holiday was over, though it had hardly begun. "We must go home," Mama kept saying, growing more agitated every time she glanced at the newspaper, or looked out of the window. "I don't feel safe here. I want us all to be at home."

Papa, too, decided that he was needed urgently at work, since the outbreak of war affected banking in ways Polly didn't understand. "We'll go tomorrow.

We'll pack up as quickly as we can, and I'll arrange train tickets."

"We're so vulnerable here." Mama could not sit still; she kept looking out at the promenade, then lowering herself into a chair, only to struggle up again a moment later. "Suppose the Germans invade? Supposing the baby's born here, with a German army in control?" .

"Catherine, please!" Papa guided her back to her seat, and handed her a glass of water. "Don't alarm yourself unnecessarily – it won't do you any good. We'll be back at home this time tomorrow. I can't see any German invaders at the moment."

He spoke flippantly, but Polly glanced out at the shining strip of sea that was visible from their first-floor room, imagining the Germans rising out of the waves, as if they had swum all the way underwater. She had never seen a German. What would they look like? She imagined them as pirates boarding a captive ship, bloodthirsty and fierce, clamping knives between their teeth. And the captive ship would be England.

All the clothes so recently unpacked were refolded and stored back in their trunks. The station was full of khaki and backpacks and men's deep voices; a train full of soldiers had just arrived. At a command from their officer, all the men shouldered their packs and fell into line, moving off towards the harbour; they would be going across to France, Papa said. There were cheers from the street at the sight of the soldiers in uniform, and some people waved Union Jacks. The atmosphere, Polly thought, was partly of celebration, partly of waiting for something to happen. A second trainload pulled in while she waited with her parents on the platform. It felt odd to be travelling in the other direction, as if they were running away from the war, while everyone else was rushing towards it.

Half an hour later she was staring out of the train window again, in a hot compartment that smelled of dust and hot cushions, and seeing all the Kent scenery again – the drowsing orchards, the grazing sheep, the oast houses. The stuffiness made her head mazy with sleep. When she snapped back awake it was to find Mama slumping sideways on her seat, and Papa bending over her in concern.

"Open the window, Polly, quickly. It's the heat – she's passed out."

He unbuttoned the cuffs of Mama's blouse, and took off his jacket to use as a pillow, lowering her to a half-lying position. Polly struggled with the window and managed to push it down so that smutty air rushed into the compartment. Mama murmured, but her eyelids stayed closed.

"Is she ill, Papa? Will she die?" Polly's voice came out very small and frightened.

"No, no, of course not. It's the heat, and the rush and excitement. We must get her home as quickly as we can – call Dr. Mayes –"

"Is it the baby? Is the baby coming early?" Polly was

rather vague about how exactly babies were born, but could see that it would take something very extraordinary to get it out of Mama and into the world as a separate human being.

"I hope not," Papa said fervently. Polly saw that he too was scared, and did not really know what to do. This in itself was so alarming that Polly felt herself trembling, close to tears.

"There's a flask of water in that travelling bag. Fetch it, please, there's a good girl." Papa was holding one of Mama's hands, and seemed unwilling to let go. "Then I want you to go along to the guard's van and explain that Mama is unwell. He can summon help when we arrive at Victoria."

By the time Polly got back from the guard's van, Mama had revived a little, enough to sit up and sip water as the familiar London buildings slid into view, and the train crossed the Thames before slowing for the terminus. At Victoria, the guard summoned a cab and supervised the loading of the luggage, while

Polly's father helped Mama into her seat. More crowds packed the station: soldiers in uniform, nurses, families waving them off.

Home had never seemed so welcoming: the house solid and calm behind its gates, Mrs. Parks in charge, everything in order. It felt to Polly as if she had never been away. Her father helped Mama to bed, and Mrs. Parks fetched cool drinks and a cold compress, while Polly tried to make herself useful by starting on the unpacking. Dr. Mayes arrived, and there was a hushed conference in the bedroom, while Polly hovered uncertainly outside the door.

"Baby's on its way," Mrs. Parks told Polly when she emerged. "A bit early, but Doctor thinks all will be well. I must boil up some hot water, and we'll need flannels, and clean towels."

"I'll fetch them," Polly offered, but at the same moment her father came out of the bedroom, looking both eager and anxious.

"Polly, I want you to go downstairs to Mrs. Dalby,

and stay there till I come and fetch you. I saw Maurice in the garden – you can go and play with him if you like."

"But –" Polly felt herself too grown-up for playing, too important to be simply got rid of. She had helped on the train, hadn't she, and at the station, with the cab and the luggage?

"Go," said her father firmly. "You'll only be in everyone's way. Your mother will be perfectly all right with Dr. Mayes to look after her. I'll come and fetch you as soon as there's any news."

"It's best you do as he says," Mrs. Parks told her in an undertone. "You go and see Maurice. Before long, you'll have a little brother or sister – won't that be exciting? And" – she checked that Papa had gone back into the bedroom, and that the door was closed – "there's news from upstairs. Miss Rutherford's back from prison, but apparently Miss Cross is moving out!"

"Moving out? Why?"

"Some argument, Kitty said. Now, you run along." Mrs. Parks shooed Polly towards the stairs.

Polly closed the door to the flat but stood on the landing, listening. Floorboards creaked from the flat above, and she heard a voice call out – Violet's? It seemed an age since she'd had any sort of proper conversation with Violet or Edwina. No one was going to take much notice of where she was, not with everyone scurrying about with compresses and towels and hot water. She went upstairs instead of down, then hesitated again at the door of Flat Three. An argument, Mrs. Parks had said? Like last time? But the voice she'd just heard didn't sound like arguing; it only sounded like Violet calling out to Edwina, in a perfectly cheerful way.

While she stood there, the door opened and Kitty came out, almost colliding with her. "Oh! I'm sorry. Do come in. We're all in a muddle."

Kitty stepped aside for Polly to enter. A suitcase stood in the hall with a furled umbrella leaning against it, and a Gladstone bag, and two small packing crates. It was true, then, what Mrs. Parks had said.

"You can keep all them posters," Violet's voice called out, "but I'm taking my banner, seeing as I wore out my fingers sewing it – oh! Polly! Thought you was at Folkestone?"

"We're back because of the war," Polly explained, "and now Mama's having the baby. The doctor's with her now. But what's happening here? Why are you leaving? It's not Mrs. Dalby, is it?"

Violet looked puzzled. "Mrs. Dalby?"

"Maurice's mother. She thought –" Polly felt awkward saying it. "She thought you and Edwina shouldn't be allowed to live here."

"Oh!" Violet seemed to think this of no consequence whatsoever. "No, no, it en't that. Come and say hello to Edwina. She's been ill again, but getting better."

Edwina was at her desk in the drawing room, sorting through papers. She looked just as thin and frail as when Polly had first met her: how could she keep on *doing* this to herself, Polly wondered?

"They let us all out of prison, because of the war," she told Polly. "So I can eat again, hoorah! And Kitty's made us a lovely cherry cake. Do stay and share it with us."

Polly was puzzled – there seemed to be no sign of another quarrel, yet it seemed that Violet was leaving, and Edwina was staying. She was halfway through her slice of cake before she plucked up courage to ask them about it. They exchanged rueful glances in the way Polly had seen before. Then Edwina replied:

"Well, Polly, you've obviously realized that Violet and I, though the best of friends, don't always see eye to eye. And especially so, now that war's broken out. The Pankhursts have split over it, and so have we. We feel quite differently about the war, and what it means for our aims. Mrs. Pankhurst has decided that all our campaigning must stop – we must support enlistment, encourage men to join the army. And besides that, we'll work, we'll work hard, whatever way we can, so the government will see just what women can do when they're given the chance. I'm going to be a volunteer nurse, and get out to France or Belgium if I can. Whereas –" She nodded to Violet, who took over.

"Back to the East End, for me. It's where I belong, and where I should be now." She smiled. "I've liked living here, and I've liked meeting you, Polly, but now I'm going back, to work with Sylvia Pankhurst. Her aims have always been a bit different from her mother's and Christabel's. Sylvia's against the war, like I am. And it's the poor that's going to suffer most, like always. She wants to help the East End families – they'll be facing a real struggle, with their men away. And that's where I'm going, too, to work in a canteen. There's so much to be done."

"Oh." Polly looked from one to the other, with the sad sense that something was coming to an end: the specialness contained in this flat, and all it had meant to her. Edwina would still be here, but it wouldn't be the same without Violet.

Violet was looking wistful, too. She reached for an old envelope from the heap of papers Edwina was sorting. "Here, I'll give you my address. Maybe you'll write?"

"Of course I will," Polly said. "And –?" She looked at Edwina.

"Oh, we'll still stay friends, Violet and I," Edwina said. "We've known each other too long to fall out completely over a difference of opinion. And we haven't got votes for women yet! Till then, there's a lot more campaigning to do."

Violet handed Polly the envelope: on it she had written *c/o Miss Sylvia Pankhurst, 400 Old Ford Road, London, E.3.* She glanced at the clock. "Time to be on my way." She stood, and shook hands formally with Polly.

"Goodbye, Violet," Polly said. "I – I'm sorry."

"So am I," Violet replied. "About this sorry mess those politicians have got us into. But sorry to be saying goodbye, Polly, too. It's been nice getting to know you a bit. Good luck to you. I hope you do whatever you want in your life."

"Get the vote," Edwina said. "And know what you want to do – be an explorer. Do it. Decide for yourself."

They were in agreement about *that*, anyway.

⁓

Feeling slightly dazed by it all, Polly wandered out into the garden. Everything was changing, she thought, and by the time she went back upstairs her family would have changed, too. There would be herself, Mama, Papa, and someone else: this unknown new person, with a whole life to live. What a strange thought that was!

"Hello, Pegs," Maurice called. Funny, but she didn't mind any more when he called her that; it sounded friendly now. He was standing underneath the walnut tree, looking up into its branches. "Look, you can see the new walnuts coming. We'll be able to eat them at Christmas."

Polly looked at the small green fruits in the lushness of leaves high above her head. She thought of the girl who had lived here, long ago, who had grown this whole tree from one walnut. Could she have ever imagined, carefully planting one shrivelled walnut in the soil, two children standing in its shade, looking up at its new crop of nuts?

"Isn't it exciting about the war?" Maurice said, turning to look at her. "You can join the army at eighteen, so I've only got five years and ten months to wait. If I go into the army I shall be an officer."

"Don't be stupid," Polly said, laughing. "The war's not going to go on for five years and ten months, is it? Everyone says it'll be over by Christmas."

Chapter Eighteen

Secrets

Dear Lily, Polly wrote. *So much has happened since I sent you the postcard from Folkestone that I hardly know where to start. Most exciting of all is that I have a brand new baby brother! He was born yesterday and his name is Edward. Till a few weeks ago Mama and Papa had thought of calling him William if he turned out to be a boy, but now of course they can't, because of Kaiser Wilhelm.*

So he is named Edward after the old King.

All the waiting time I was hoping he would be a girl, but after all I am quite pleased to have a brother.

Polly had not realized this until writing it down. It was another of the surprising changes that yesterday had brought.

BC

The baby had taken so long being born that Polly had stayed for supper with the Dalbys and played two games of chess with Maurice on the landing, losing both times, because Maurice was rather good at chess. "It's like war," he told her. "All about manoeuvres and stealth."

It was almost bedtime before Mrs. Parks came down with the news. "You've got a new baby brother! Come up and meet him!"

"A boy! Oh, what wonderful news!" Mrs. Dalby clapped her hands. "There, didn't I tell you it would be a boy? Your father will be so delighted!"

But Polly, not delighted at all, had felt a lump of sourness inside her as she climbed the stairs as slowly as she could – a lump that stuck in her throat and would hardly let her swallow.

"Come along!" Mrs. Parks urged, as if the new baby were already so important that he mustn't be kept waiting five minutes.

In the bedroom, Mama smiled wearily from her propped-up pillows. "Here he is! Come and see." She was holding a white bundle that looked too tiny to be a baby. Polly bent over to look, and saw a small red face bunched up tightly, an almost cross expression, and a hand with tiny, tiny fingernails.

"Oh!" She couldn't help it; she heard the adoring note in her voice she had heard other people use when they looked at babies.

Papa was sitting in a chair beside the bed. "Meet your big sister!" he told the baby, in a funny, crooning voice Polly couldn't remember him ever using before. "She's going to be a very important person in your life."

Mama reached up her spare hand to pull Polly towards her for a kiss and a one-armed hug. "He's a very lucky baby, to have the best sister in the world! Would you like to hold him?"

He is so beautiful, Polly wrote. *Have you ever held a new baby? I hadn't, and it was amazing. He is so little and so light to hold, but then he wriggled and I could feel how strong and alive he is. His eyes are open but he doesn't even know how to see things yet. Isn't it amazing to think of all the things he will have to learn?*

Mama gave a tired smile, settling her head comfortably against the pillows. "Thank you, darling."

"What for?" Polly couldn't think of anything that deserved thanks.

"For being so good." Mama tried to stifle a yawn. "So helpful and considerate. You know you really can be such a good girl, when you want to be."

Well, yes. It was funny, Polly thought, how grown-ups sometimes said what was not quite what they meant, but was truer than what they'd intended to say. Yes, when I want to be; but that isn't always.

"What is it, Polly?" said Mama, who was sometimes very good at knowing when Polly was hiding something. Papa had gone into the drawing room to start writing cards to all the relations with news of the baby's arrival.

"It's – well, I –" Polly did not know how to put it, but came straight out with, "I expect you and Papa are very pleased to have a boy, because you'd have been disappointed if it had been another girl, wouldn't you?" It sounded like an accusation. "I mean, everyone says, at least Mrs. Dalby does, that a boy would be best."

"Polly! Is that what you've been worrying about?" Mama said gently. "Yes, we're delighted to have a boy, because now we're very lucky to have a son *and* a lovely daughter. But you mustn't ever think we love one of you more than the other! Promise me you will never believe that?"

"The way Papa talked to the baby just now!" Polly said, to avoid answering. "I don't believe he ever talked to me like that!"

"Polly," Mama said firmly. "When you were born, your father was the proudest man in London. He told me he felt as if he could leap the River Thames in one bound or jump up and swing from the hands of Big Ben. And he still is, Polly – as proud of his daughter as I am."

Mama and I have a secret, now, Polly wrote. *I didn't think Mama ever had secrets from Papa, but she does, and this is it.*

"He gets such an unfair start, being a boy!" Now that Polly had started, something seemed to be pushing her to say more and more, all the things she had kept inside for so long. "I'm only a girl, so I have to be ladylike, and do what I'm told, and behave nicely, and have other people decide for me. He's only just born, but he'll be able to vote when he's grownup, and boss people about, and think himself better than me!"

"But, Polly, darling!" Mama rocked the baby gently in her arms. "Things are changing now, for women especially. You'll have the vote when you're old enough, I'm certain – thanks to the efforts of people like Miss Rutherford and Miss Cross, and their determination –"

"Mama!" Polly was astonished. "I thought you disapproved of them!"

Mama smiled. "I disapprove of some of the things they do. Your father disapproves of them, certainly. But –" She glanced at the closed door. "Perhaps this had better be our secret, Polly. I also admire them. I admire them for standing up for what they believe in, and for fighting for it. They are so brave, so determined not to give in! I could never do that myself, but I'm very glad there are people who do."

So, who would have guessed it? My mother a secret suffragette sympathizer! And now that we've got one secret, we can have more – that I shall write to Violet in the Old Ford Road, and even go to visit if I can. I have written her new address in the marbled notebook you gave me, which I use for my Plans and Ideas. My Plans and Ideas will have to be secret, but I will share them with you.

Papa sets the rules of the house, but he cannot tell me what to think. Mama always does what he says, because he is her husband and she promised to obey him and that is what everyone expects. But things are changing, even Mama says so. Things will be different when we grow up. I'm going to be an explorer, and by then I expect women will be able to do all sorts of things they don't do now. Papa will have to get used to it.

He is so pleased and relieved about the baby, and that Mama is recovering well, that she thinks if I explain to him again about Hyde Park, and make him understand that it really was all my idea, not yours or Aunt Dorothy's, he will change his mind about the piano lessons, and will let me come to stay with you. Except now of course there's the war and that changes things again, because who knows what will happen? Maybe I'll be allowed to be friends with Edwina, too, now that she's giving up campaigning, to support the war effort. Papa can't object to that, can he?

So for now I shall have to make do with Maurice. But that's another strange thing — I have decided that Maurice isn't so bad after all, even if he does always beat me at chess. I think I will have to be truthful and say that I <u>like</u> him.

Isn't it amazing how people can keep surprising you?

CB

Author's note

It was our editor who had the clever idea of publishing three stories set in the same house, at different times. From then on, we three authors had great fun deciding where "our" house should be, how it should look, inside and out, and how it would change as the years went by. That made it very interesting, once I'd written *Polly's March*, to read the stories written by my two friends – especially as I bumped into one of my own characters, Edwina, who reappears in Ann's story, *Josie Under Fire*!

It took me no time at all to decide that my story would be set in 1914 – the campaign for Votes for Women is something I've always wanted to write about. At twelve, Polly is too young to be a suffragette, but she is greatly impressed by Edwina and Violet, the older girls who move in upstairs.

By now, No. 6, Chelsea Walk really does feel like a house I've lived in myself. Who knows – maybe I'll have the chance to revisit it in another story?

Linda Newbery

About the author

Linda Newbery is the successful author of over twenty books for children and teenagers. She was first inspired to write when teaching English at a secondary school. Her novels have garnered much critical acclaim and *The Shell House* and *Sisterland* have both been shortlisted for the Carnegie Medal.

Linda lives with her husband and three cats in Northamptonshire.

To find out more about Linda Newbery, you can visit her website: www.lindanewbery.co.uk.

Usborne Quicklinks

For links to interesting websites where you can find out more about the suffragette movement, play a game about women's rights, and listen to soldiers describe their experiences in the First World War, go to the Usborne Quicklinks website at www.usborne-quicklinks.com and enter the keyword "polly".

Internet safety

When using the Internet, make sure you follow these safety guidelines:

- Ask an adult's permission before using the Internet.
- Never give out personal information, such as your name, address or telephone number.
- If a website asks you to type in your name or email address, check with an adult first.
- If you receive an email from someone you don't know, don't reply to it.

Mary Ann & Miss Mozart
1764
Ann Turnbull

Mary Ann's greatest wish is to become an opera singer, but when she is told she must leave her Boarding School for Young Ladies, her singing dreams are shattered. Distraught, she comes up with a plan to stay at school, oblivious to the danger it will put her in...

ISBN 9780746073117

Lizzie's Wish
1857
Adèle Geras

When Lizzie's stepfather sends her to stay with relatives in London, Lizzie struggles to adapt to her new life of stiff manners and formal pastimes. She lives for the daily letters from her mother, but when the letters suddenly stop, Lizzie sets out to discover the truth and finds herself on a rescue mission.

ISBN 0 7460 6030 0

Cecily's Portrait
1895
Adèle Geras

Cecily is enchanted when she meets Rosalind, a photographer, who seems to be the perfect match for Cecily's lonely widowed father. But her father's friend, the dull and dowdy Miss Braithwaite, keeps spoiling her plans to unite the pair. Will Cecily's dreams ever come true?

ISBN 9780746073124

Polly's March
1914
LINDA NEWBERY

When Polly discovers her new neighbours are suffragettes, fighting for women's right to vote, she is determined to join their protest march. But her parents are scandalized. Will she dare to defy them and do what she thinks is right?

ISBN 0 7460 6031 9

ભ

Josie Under Fire
1941
ANN TURNBULL

When Josie goes to stay with her cousin, Edith, she tries to fit in by joining Edith and her friends in teasing a timid classmate. But when the bullying gets out of hand, Josie faces a dilemma: she knows what it feels like to be picked on, but if she takes a stand, will Edith tell everyone her secret?

ISBN 0 7460 6032 7

ભ

Andie's Moon
1969
LINDA NEWBERY

Andie dreams of becoming an artist and loves living in Chelsea, with the fashion, music and art galleries along the trendy King's Road. There's even a real artist living in the flat downstairs. Could Andie's paintings, inspired by the excitement of the first-ever moon landing, be good enough to win his approval?

ISBN 9780746073100